TABASCO

TABASCO

JOHN B. THOMPSON

CUTTING EDGE

ISBN-13: 978-1-962896-41-2

Published by
Cutting Edge Books
PO Box 8212
Calabasas, CA 91372
www.cuttingedgebooks.com

CHAPTER ONE

THE EXPERIENCE of losing a woman to the trials and pressures of the times was something not in the least new to Donald Ransom Gerdt. It had happened to him twice during World War II and now that he was back from Korea, never more to fly in the wars, it had happened again. Nor was woman trouble the worst of his trials. He had been branded a hero, and to Don Gerdt there was nothing worse than to be placed on a rostrum with noisy bellowing politicians, made over and looked upon as a major deity.

As he sat at the bar, his lean six feet plus still showing the need for the flesh he had lost, he let his mind wander for the fiftieth time over the circumstances that had made a hero of him.

It was a bitter cold day and Korean weather was really putting on a show for the benefit of airmen. Don was flying a Corsair in support of the Marine evacuation of the Chosin Reservoir when a shell fragment from ground fire tore into his engine. Grabbing all the altitude he could, he headed back for the *Roanoke,* his body tense, nerves centered on fighting the crippled plane whose every move was bringing him closer to the snow covered terrain beneath.

The beach ahead looked as good as the motor sounded bad but in a matter of a few seconds he discovered that the worst sounding motor is better than the chill silence that sprang suddenly into being as the power plant quit cold. The wailing of the wind was all the comfort he had. That and the fact that he was now over the water and safe from enemy ground forces.

He looked at the water as it came up much too fast, at a nearby communist-held island and the boats in the tiny harbor that were firing at him wildly.

"Bastards," he commented grittily and, swinging the Corsair toward them, fed them a taste of twenty millimeter projectiles, spraying out the last rounds as impartially as he could. He tried to nurse the nose up and land on the beach but he had lost too much altitude and speed.

The heavy ship began to yaw and Don, who flew a lot by the seat of his pants felt a swift chill flit through his limbs. Seconds later the warning became fact and the stricken fighter grazed a small patrol vessel, caromed off, struck another, skated on the water in two bone-wrenching smacks, rammed up on the beach and shed its wings as it hurtled between two boulders, then the plane cartwheeled and came to rest against another boulder, bursting into a blob of red flame. The cartwheel had thrown him clear but the impact was not conducive to clear thinking.

The first soldier to reach him was armed with a submachine gun and advanced with visions of fame for bringing in an American flyer. No sane man would have done what Don then did. He sat up, shook his head, got to his feet and with a quick step forward reached out and snatched the sub-gun from the man's cold, numbed fingers and smashed him in the face with the butt. He bent over and took spare clips which he thrust in the pockets of his flying suit and from then on all was a nightmare. With a sort of somnambulistic disregard for the finer points of safety he marched, gun flaming, through the ten men who were hurrying to assist their fellow, leaving them kicking on the frozen sand. A larger group charged him, but with seven of their members down they took to the rocks firing freely but inaccurately. He marched steadily on until a curve in the beach took him from their sight.

Fifteen minutes later he appeared out of the thickening mist in a small boat, like a ghost, shot every man on deck of a patrol vessel and then clambered aboard, much to the intense relief of three Americans who were manacled to the boat's engines below decks. Their four communist guards, seeing that this madman ignored their first shots and was deliberately preparing to plaster them all over the cockpit, screamed for mercy at the top of their voices and threw away their weapons. One he shot anyway because he seemed reluctant to part with his piece. The others were immediately impressed into service and the boat began to pick up speed, being fired upon without apparent effect by every other boat within sight. Then the mist rolled in thickly and blotted them from view. Several hours later they were ordered to heave to or be blown out of the water by a PT boat. Finding out who they were, the boat escorted them to the *Roanoke* and, with a sharp turn to port, disappeared in a swirl of foam and fog.

Then in the ward room surrounded by buddies and brass whose rank prevented them from being buddies, Don gradually came back to consciousness. He had seven holes in his flying togs, three of which had bitten away enough skin to bring blood. Otherwise, except for a nasty bump on the back of his head, he was all right.

Bucky Walters smote him a hard blow on the shoulders. "Boy, you're a bleedin' hero. We got the whole story from those guys you rescued. They were on the deck of that little patrol craft. They had been captured, returning from a C and D mission with their pants loaded with secrets. They were on deck when you started toward the craft but when the reds saw that a bullet couldn't hit you they took these guys below deck."

Don blinked his eyes dully. "What the hell are you talking about?"

A silence fell on the assembly. "You mean you don't—" Bucky massaged his chin. "Look, fella, modesty is all right but—"

"Look yourself," snapped Don angrily. "I cracked up on one of those harbor boats, then I skated a couple of bumps on the water, skidded up on the beach and from there on I don't remember a thing. I don't know what you're talking about." He got up and glared around. "And knock off this hero stuff. If it's some-one's idea of a bad joke I fail to catch the humor."

Major Pittman, fat and yet hard, surged forward. "Are you serious, Gerdt?"

Don's face, worn and haggard, tightened. "You heard me, didn't you?"

Then Colonel Beatty approached. "Do you mean to say you have no recollection of your actions for the past few hours, Gerdt?"

"That's right, sir."

The old man shook his gray head. "Beats anything I ever heard of. Unintentional hero."

"If I may say so, sir," put in Bucky Walters, "it may have been unconscious but it wasn't unintentional. I know this guy. That's just what he would have done if he'd been conscious."

"Oh, why don't you shut up," flared Don tiredly. "If you think I'd take a small boat and row out to a patrol craft with them shooting at me every step you're a jackass."

"And all along the shore," cried the Army Major, one of the three he had rescued. "They shot at you, dozens of them, and you never stopped walking. Those that charged you, you mowed down. I never saw anything like it."

"You should be a Marine," chuckled Colonel Beatty, and the Major grinned back. "I've done all the talking about the Marines I'm going to. From now on they're my special pets."

"Tell the Pentagon that," said the Colonel with a smile.

The Major stood up and, palming something, shoved it at the Colonel, who was visibly impressed. "Don't think I won't, sir!" Don Gerdt felt his heart sink, it did not play him any more false than the warning chill that swept him just before the Corsair went into the drink.

By the time the story reached the newspapers, Don was left without his only defense—that he had been unconscious throughout the whole affair.

The last thing Colonel Beatty said to him was: "Gerdt, for God's sake don't go back to the States with that absurd tale about being unconscious. Someone might think you were breaking your back to be modest."

The shell fragment had proved troublesome and as a result Don nearly lost his leg. He had hobbled through the ceremony at the White House, had accepted the medal from a man whom he heartily disliked, and had promptly passed out on the carpet, waking up in the National Naval Medical Center several days later.

They saved his leg, but they couldn't save him from the home town folks and now he sat in a bar about one-third crocked, hoping it was all over, but feeling that it probably wasn't.

"Know just how you feel, boy," rasped Rusty McCraine, the bartender. "I won me a Silver Star in the Sea Bees last war and they likened to heckled the tail off me. All I done was cover up some Jap fox holes with a bulldozer to keep the bastards from killin' me."

"That," said Don pounding his fist on the bar, "is my point. This hero stuff makes me tired. How many people did you ever see who went out to be a hero? Not a damn one. A man gets in a tight spot and manages to get the hell out of it the best way he can and what happens? Hero!" He spat disgustedly. "Hero be damned. I got a conk on the onion and pulled a lot of fool stunts, and I do mean fool stunts, like I was taking a stroll down Main Street. That sound like a man in his right mind? Had seven holes in my flying suit. Seven, mind you, and three of them drew blood but that was all. Hero! Gimme another straight with coke."

A group of people came in and one of them detached himself from the group and pounced on Don. It was Abel Hackett, son of the town's rich man, the banker. Abel was a lawyer and had held a soft job in the Judge Advocate's office in Washington during the last war.

"Well, Don, how does it feel to be the town's hero—" He stopped because a hand driven with lip-splitting force cracked into his mouth. He reeled back and put his hand to his mouth.

"Why, you—"

"I hope you do," said Don cuttingly, "you swivel chair soldier. I'm fed to the teeth with this muck and I'd as soon take you apart as look at you. Rather, in fact. You never liked me and I never liked you. Nothing's changed —sonny!"

"What's the matter, Abel?" asked another of the group who, seeing the blood on Abel's shirt front, came over.

"Our hero is touchy," said Abel, panting heavily, trying to keep his temper.

"Maybe he needs working over," suggested David Pratt, a chunky lawyer who wore glasses.

"Maybe you'd like to try it," said Don, getting off his stool. "Call the rest of 'em over and make it interesting, why don't you?"

"Yeah," rumbled Rusty, easing his bulk out from behind the bar, "bring 'em all over. I think the Navy and Marines can handle 'em."

Their exit was not hasty, but on the other hand they didn't let time creep up on them.

"You should have stayed behind the bar, Rusty," said Don slumping on his stool. "This is your living."

"Not them. That's the Country Club crowd. They don't buy enough here to pay my sandwich bill."

"Set 'em up again."

"Sure. This one's on the house."

Don looked morosely into his glass and thought about Kathleen. She had been different and in spite of his previous experience he left for Korea with the feeling that here at last was one girl he could trust to wait for him.

When he got back she was all smiles and honey and he thought he had picked up where he left off.

Then came the night when he arrived home from a trip to Washington a day early. He had left his baggage at his aunt's house and walked three blocks to the big house where Kathleen lived.

It was nine o'clock but he was sure she would still be awake. She was, but not unattended. He had watched and listened from the protection of a hedge while Laughton Herrin and Kathleen performed for him.

"You've got to tell him sooner or later," Laughton had protested.

"Later, darling… " She leaned forward and kissed him. "Later. Right now I'm enjoying all the adulation and rounds of lights and laughter."

He caught her close and in the bright light of the moon not only kissed her but essayed some bold and flesh-revealing exploration. She did not object and the throaty gurgle that came from her lips, the clutch of her arms about his neck and the subtle assistance which her body performed, made sweat start out on Don's forehead. Her father was deaf, he remembered, and an early-to-bed believer. Protected from the house by shrubs, they were safe. She was now in a very vulnerable position and Laughton was kissing her in a way that made Her whimper with urgency.

With a muttered curse Don turned on his heel and stalked off, the mating note from her throat seeming to -follow him long after he was out of hearing.

"Women," he said to the drink before him which seemed to leer.

"Bight," said Rusty. "Melt 'em all together and what you got? A bed job, a bad cook or a passel of trouble. They ain't worth it."

"Brother, you said that right."

"Another one?"

"Sure. 'Nother one, then 'nother. Plenty of 'em."

"What you going to do now, Don?"

"Get drunk," said the other without raising his head.

"I mean for a living."

"Hell, who cares? I don't know. I got an aunt that feeds good."

"That don't get it."

"Yeah, I know. I hadn't thought about it. Need a helper?"

Rusty chuckled dryly. "How long a up-and-comin' lad like you would last in here?"

"How long would a up-and-comin' drunk last anywhere?"

"You're no drunk. Come the day when all these birds get out of your hair you'll be right back to social drinkin'."

Don passed a numb hand over his almost kinky black hair, as though to hasten the process. "Got to do something, though. Pension's not enough. Saved a little while I was in action. No place to spend it."

"I used to gamble with mine," said Rusty. "Won thirty thousand in three years."

"Craps?"

"Nope. Poker. That's a science, poker is, and I'm one of the best."

"You play it straight?"

"Long's the other guys do. I can pull some tricks if I have to."

"Sounds like a good racket."

"Science. I don't have the bug like it's got some people. I can leave it alone."

"I think I'm silly sitting here getting drank."

"Sure you are. No need to let them people make you do yourself a bad turn."

"Ri'! So I'm gonna show 'em. I'm goin' home."

"That's the boy. Want one for traveling?"

"Yeah, short one." He downed the drink, pulled himself together with an effort and went out into the cool spring night. The moon shone down brightly as he walked along the oak-shaded sidewalk, not too steadily.

At an intersection he stopped to let a light cream Packard convertible pass but instead of passing it stopped.

"Going some place, hero?"

He blinked at the girl driving and frowned. "Not with you, bitch—you and your hero stuff."

"Oh, come now. I used it sarcastically. I know how you feel and I promise not to use it any more."

By this time he realized that he was faced with something rare in feminine architecture. She was one of those magnificent copper blondes with skin as rich as Jersey cream, tanned and chested like Venus. She was long of leg and lean of flank, this being obvious because she wore only close-fitting white shorts and a scarlet halter. Over the shorts was a skirt of the same material but it was unbuttoned and open.

"Do I pass?"

"What? Oh. I'm sorry." All of a sudden he seemed to feel the kindness of her reach out and envelope him in a humid fragrant cloud. He grinned. "You pass. In fact, you had me gawking. I'm sorry."

"You can skip the sorrow. I know I'm sort of fetchin' to the eye and I like it. In fact, I wallow in it. Want a lift?"

"How do you know I'm going your way?"

"I don't have any way. I'm just riding."

He opened the door and sat beside her. "Let's ride, then. I left a bar to keep from getting drunk."

"Shucks," she said as the car purred smoothly away, "and I wanted to get drunk."

"What are you running from?"

"Maybe the same thing you're running from. Eyes. Eyes all around, nasty-minded men, vicious yakkity bitches of women."

He chuckled dryly. "You're not put together in a manner designed to keep men in the best state of mind."

"You don't get me. When you stared at me back there it was different."

"How?"

"Yours was honest, straightforward admiration set in motion by a healthy set of glands. What I mean is men whose mind only carries filth. Who'd yank the pants off every female they could and advertise it the next day, half of which advertisement would be a lie."

"Maybe I'm that way."

"Maybe, but if you are then I don't know anything about people. I was at the Kiwanis dinner and the Polo Club dinner too. I saw you, but you didn't see me. I was so furious at those politicians I got up and left."

"You were lucky. I was stuck."

"Yes, and when you told the mayor you'd throw him through the wall if he didn't lay off the local boy hero stuff, through the nearest wall, you meant it. I knew you meant it and I was on your side."

"Sure, you and who else?" He scratched his head in perplexity. "By the way, you're being pretty swell about this. What, if any, is the pitch?"

"No pitch, Don. I was lonely tonight for a man who didn't have a set of figures for a mind and a latrine for a soul. To be short and to the point, I was looking for you. I left home early and I rode until I saw you come out of the bar. I missed you on two corners and finally caught you where I picked you up."

"You're good people," he said huskily, touching her bare shoulder and feeling the magnificent muscles leap under his touch. "I needed you like a drowning man needs a raft, like a dip needs a bottle, like a snifter needs a touch of snow. That is, if you don't skate away in the fog, leaving me waked up and cursing because it and you and this whole lovely improbable thing is a figment of a dream. Not that it matters but you know something that just popped into my head, I don't even know your name."

"I'm Cassandra Caraway and don't call me Cassy."

"Ah. Now I see a lot I didn't see."

"I thought you would."

"Tell me about it."

"There's nothing much to tell. I came from Brownsville, met my husband in Austin when I played in a tennis tournament while I was at Texas U. A year ago he was killed in a plane crash arid left me loaded."

"I knew something about that," he said, lighting a cigarette and passing it to her. He lit one for himself and sank back against the rich upholstery. "What was the talk about you and Abel Hackett?"

Her lips compressed. "That was what I meant about dirty men. I shouldn't have gone out with him in the first place, but I was lonely and about to snap. We got tight and it happened, then I became very popular all of a sudden. In a pattern. It got nosed about and now I'm the fallen woman who went hunting before my husband was cold. You know the line."

"I know it," he replied grimly. "I should."

"I thought you would. So since I'm already a fallen woman I brazenly set out to stalk you."

"To what end? Say, don't you have a more easily handled name?"

"I have a middle name you might like—Dariel. An old Mexican nurse gave me that one. I never heard it before. And about the end. I don't know. I just thought you might be interested."

"I'm afraid I'm too radical to be interested. People bore the tail off me, unless I pick them."

"Well, you surely didn't pick me."

He laughed. "I'll forget that. Seems you're about as good at picking as I am. And where are we headed?"

"I have a camp out on Lake Poule D'eau."

"You really must be loaded. What's the camp like?"

"Pretty big and I have a bar, a boat and a private wharf. I still want to get drunk."

"I'm nearly sober and it takes a lot to send me, so lead on. I haven't felt this good since I got back."

"That sounded like a compliment, Don."

"That's the way I intended it."

They were silent for a while and he stole glances at the firm flesh of her straight strong legs, slim waist and the cliffs of her high assertive breasts. She was a big girl but quantity hadn't been any obstacle to quality.

She laughed softly. "I must be good to look at."

"Have you ever doubted it?"

"Yes. When I was twelve I was all legs, eyes and hair."

"You still have enough hair to stuff a mattress. Shake it down."

She loosened a pin or two and shook her head. The copper gold masses fell to her shoulders and began to shimmer in the moonlight as the wind whipped them about. "Like it?"

"Love it," he said, his voice soft and gentle. "I'd like to get my hands in it."

"What will you give me if I let you?"

"I think the knowledge of what you'll be giving me will be enough reward."

She looked at him quickly. "Oh. Don, I knew there was something batting around in my head. You're the one Kathleen Morrison is engaged to, aren't you?"

"Was," he corrected harshly. "It seems that while I was gone Laughton Herrin was making hay."

"I know. And yet when you came back she was all ready with an act. I hate her."

"I guess I did too for a while, but what the hell. I've been scarred up so much that once more doesn't seem to make any difference."

"You've been hurt," she said so gently that his heart ached with a sudden fierce affection.

"Yes, I've been hurt, but somehow you've stepped into the breach and now it doesn't seem important. Not as important as, say, filling my hands with that beautiful fine hair and smelling the faint perfume it must have."

"I've been hurt, too," she said after a time. "Maybe we were drawn together because of it. There's the camp."

It was a low rambling structure built very near the shore and one could walk from the front porch down to the water without ever touching the ground. There was a boathouse connected and he could hear the creak of the craft as it leaned against the rubber bumpers.

"Looks like you have everything here," he said. "Even a boat."

"Even a boat. A thirty-foot Chris Craft and can it skim the water. Want a ride?"

"After a few drinks. My buzz is running down."

They went into the camp house where he was pleasantly surprised by the tremendous living room. There were deer hides on the floor, keeping company with Navajo rugs, and colorful blankets that had been carelessly thrown over heavy comfortable couches. There was a big radio in one corner with a phonograph attachment which she immediately set in action.

He watched the elegant structure of her hands as she twirled dials and set the records in place. Her fingers were long and tapering with nails that had been carefully tended and lacquered a brilliant red. Her wrists were strong, making him remember that she played tennis. The calves of her legs were strong and shapely like her thighs but her ankles were as slim and delicate as a dancer's. Strength, he thought. Not brute, ox-like strength but the finely turned strength of a blooded horse. She turned and intercepted his rapt gaze.

"Look here, lad, I'll start getting the swelled head if you don't stop devouring me like that."

"You're the most delightfully contrived bit of female architecture I ever saw," he said seriously. "I'm sorry if I gawk, but I just can't help it."

She stared at him for a moment, then swiftly and impulsively she walked over and kissed him gently on the lips. "Don't even try to help it," she said, her voice soft with feeling, then she laughed. "How did we ever proceed at this speed? What sort of people are we?"

"People who've been hurt. We salve each other." He reached up and filled his hands with her thick hair and massaged it gently. "Nothing on earth like it," he murmured ecstatically. "Nothing."

She caught his wrists with her hands and stroked them impartially with her soft cheeks. "You're good for me, Don, so very good for me. I've needed you a long, long time."

The touch of her hair on his palms wrenched the nerves of his arms into spasms. Acting on the strength of a furious driving impulse, he pulled her to him by the hair and kissed her long with an ardor that gathered force and heat until when they finally broke they were gasping and their bodies filled with a strange wonderous longing.

"Don, that was sweet, so sweet."

"Go start the phonograph, darling," he said with a quaver to his voice. "I can take just so much of this, then I go wild and start eating the furniture."

She shook her hair back. The movement made her skirt come apart and exposed a length of richly tanned thigh; it stretched the fine skin of her stomach and lifted her breasts into prominence. He could tell then that their own lusty compactness, the solidity of the marvelous flesh, was all the support they had. His mouth went suddenly dry.

"Now," she said with a sigh as she turned to the phonograph. "I'm wondering if this is good."

"How?" he asked.

"Good for me—good for us. We strike fire too easily, Don. I'm beginning to be afraid."

She started the machine; from its expensive insides, rich rhythm began to flood forth. She turned around, her eyes questioning and her lips faintly tremulous. "Do you see what I mean?"

He grinned. "Look, Dariel, let's get unserious and have a drink. I feel it just like you do and I guess I should be concerned. The old me would. Now I find I'm startled out of myself by the wonder of you and eager to know you and what goes on under that lovely hair. Maybe it is dangerous, but aren't most worthwhile things? Right now, I feel that I wouldn't have missed this for all the tea in China, even if it does hurt later."

She caught her breath. "That's telling me, Don. What am I looking a gift horse in the mouth for? Borrowing trouble! I'll get drinks."

She opened a portable bar near the phonograph and while she mixed drinks she moved her lithe body to the tempo of the music, her hips rolling with sinuous subtlety. Her back was a broad flawless field of tan, the skin as smooth as satin, long rippling muscles restless beneath its surface. She brought the drinks and they sat on the low couch. With a hidden switch she dimmed the lights and they drank in close, intimate silence for a while.

"What do you intend to do now, Don? I mean after your doting public forgets you?"

He grimaced and wiped sweat from the sides of the aluminum tumbler. "I haven't given it much thought. I was with an insurance firm as an adjuster. It wasn't bad and it wasn't good. I don't think I'll go back."

"I can't picture you in such a job," she murmured, running the tip of her red tongue around the rim of the glass, an act that gave him a strange thrill. Her eyes, he saw, were grey-green; the lids were as smooth as mother of pearl, almost translucent, and the lashes were abnormally long, silky and darker than her hair. Her face had been cast in a mold of classic proportion, but it was not a mechanical sort of face, rather the opposite. It could light up like a bulb, become serious, vixenish, and laughter came easily to her full red lips.

"I feel I'm getting the eye again," she said with a smile.

"That's a safe assumption any time," he reminded her. "Especially when I'm around."

Three drinks later her eyes began to glisten and full-throated laughter came more often. She squirmed around, sliding both legs through the opening in the skirt, and leaned against the far end of the couch. Though the shorts fit well, from this vantage point he could see the frothy suggestion of white briefs peeking through the narrow opening. She leaned back forcing her breasts upward and they seemed determined to tear away the frail confinement. He swallowed the last of his drink, leaned over and kissed her just below the halter at the depression between her breasts. A little gurgle sounded in her throat and she arched herself further back. Her stomach flattened, the edges of her ribs appeared, padded with fine flesh, and her graceful hands knotted tightly.

"I'll have another," he said with a calm he did not feel. "What about you?"

"Hurry." She was breathless and not because she needed a drink.

CHAPTER TWO

H E BROUGHT it and she drank it down in four swift gulps. "Watch it," he warned. "I slugged it."

She put the glass down and coiled like a snake. "Who cares. I feel free in this place. No one to spy. No one to interfere, no one to disapprove. That is, unless you're in a disapproving mood."

"I'm a part of this," he told her, "and I rarely disapprove of me." He could see where she was headed and applauded her open objectivity. There was none of the tease about her.

She remained silent while he devoted his attention to his drink, striving to keep the heavy rhythm of the music out of his system for a while longer. His drinks were mounting and with them a feeling of power, shaking off the deadening tension his past troubles had produced. It was a soaring feeling, a feeling of losing the duller elements of reality and substituting in their place a glittery array of irresponsible impulses, sensing as he did that she would be with him no matter what. True, things just didn't happen this way. But he shrugged. She wasn't like the average female whose behavior had given rise to the trite conclusion that things had to happen in a certain given order. In the case of some women and some men, but not Don and Dariel.

"What are you thinking, Don?"

"I was thinking that I'd like to drag you over here by the hair and play strange music on you. You remind me of a Stradivarius that grew into a cello. You should produce exquisite music."

"I can in the hands of a master. Are you one?"

"The nearest practical thing to one."

She got to her knees and tossed her hair over her face toward him with an audible swish. "Then what are you waiting for?"

He reached out, filled his hands with her hair and gently tugged her off balance so that she fell forward into his arms. There she lay relaxed but expectant, her lips quivering slightly. And the devastating promises that shone from his face seemed to darken her eyes.

His kiss released the tigress in her and he soon found that what he had recognized as signs of strength were exactly as he had thought.

She shuddered hard as they parted to breathe, sat up and tossed her hair back with a motion of head and hands. "The only thing wrong with this," she whispered, "is the unbelievable rightness of it. Don, you're the only man who ever kissed me into a state that from another would have meant a lot of activity that you didn't have to perform. My kind of heaven isn't usually reached that way."

"You mean—"

"Yes. For a moment there I went quite blind and insane. What sort of man are you?"

"Only the promised master you asked about. If you think it was heaven I'll have to point out that it was just a whistle stop."

She grinned through the miasma of passion that he had cooled momentarily with his kisses, then initiated again without even trying. "This I must see."

"This, you will see, but we aren't adolescents operating against time. My watch says twelve o'clock and if you're seen coming into town on the heels of the sun —remember, you're a fallen woman already."

"If the stop could only be as attractive as the fall. This is Saturday night and I don't even care if I never go back to town. That's the beauty of having money. I don't have to."

"Time means little to me too, although I'm not backed up in the First National as deeply as you. I just don't give a damn."

She stood up and with a yank disposed of the skirt, sending it flying across the room. "At times like these I hate clothes. Another drink?"

"The oxygen consumed during that last breathing exercise set me back. Make it a good one."

She made two and walked back, swaying in rhythm to the music, exaggerating the motion of her hips with such primitive abandon that his back ached with tension by the time she handed him the drink.

She tasted hers, then leaned over and kissed him with hot clinging pressure. She drew away. "There's no hurry, is there?"

"Only slightly. My kisses don't do to me what they do to you. You're ahead of me."

"I'm going to stay that way," she said with a rigor that pebbled her skin with goose flesh.

"Isn't that halter cutting you?"

"No. Shall I take it off?"

"Not yet. As you said, there's no hurry. Past a certain point I don't trust myself. All in good time. Besides, I'm rather handy at such things."

"I'll bet you are. Dance?"

"I've been waiting for you to ask me."

"Swine." She bounced up and held out her hands with their glittering nails and slender fingers. He caught them, pulled himself up and they drifted away across the smooth floor. She was a dancer of the sort he liked. Steady, solid, but velvet smooth and effortless to lead. There was, he thought, an exaggeration of movement in places but the increase of her breath told its story and he smiled inwardly. There was only a thin line separating hurry from the professed lack of it.

Suddenly she stopped. "Don, kiss me. Hard."

He did and she flowed into his every outline like soft, damp, dough, sheeting over him a scattering of tiny icy darts. Her breasts were telescoped back into themselves but he was acutely conscious of their restless pressure.

She was strong and avid and stormy from the flaming desire which his kisses sent roaring into being, then she was limp and her mouth lax as she seemed to lose consciousness. He half carried her back to the couch and eased her on the upholstery. "Not again?"

She nodded jerkily and clung to him for a while. "Please, Don, don't leave me. Hold me, please. This can't be, but it is." She wept silently for a while, then held her head up, smiling, her eyes floating in twin crystal baths. "You utter—" She shook her head, making her hair dance. "You utter man!"

He got up and handed her the unfinished drink and took his own.

"To a man named Don, the incomparable," she toasted.

"To Dariel—who, if she doesn't watch out, will be calling me a harem hero or some such."

"I wish I'd thought of that," she said, squirming on the couch.

He slid a huge Navajo rug over in front of them, took off his sport shirt and sprawled out on it. She stretched out on her stomach and reached down to tousle his hair. "Lonesome so far away?"

"Yeah. Whatcha been gone so long for?"

She rolled off the couch and stroked his chest with her cheeks, her hands clenching his sides painfully. Her mouth sought his, her hair inundating them both in a sweet smother of sensation.

He released her and after a few swift productive motions their skin met from chin to ankle, embraced and almost drove consciousness from their minds with the leaping dynamic shock.

He had had reason to admire her magnificent strength, but it was nothing compared to this. She was a naiad and a python, a nymph and a wolf combining the softest touch with the most savage clonic effort. He had admired the classic cut of her legs with their suggested strength, but now he knew and times were that she almost made him cry out.

He had admired the round symmetry of her arms but now they were steel bands, then feathery wings of a butterfly that alternately caressed him with a gesture of abject adoration, then almost cut the breath from him winding about his back like hawsers of wire. Her mouth was a cup of the sweetest honey, then her teeth would sink into his shoulder without bringing blood because she'd always take in too much flesh to bite effectively.

Grey dawn peeked in the east windows when they awakened, still entwined, still welded into a single unit that even in repleteness was loath to give up what it had attained.

"Been awake long?" he asked gently.

"Not too long," a long shuddery sigh shook her. "I've been trying to think of something to say. Something that would indicate, however clumsily, how it was … but I can't. I choke up and get all overwhelmed when I try."

"Don't you think I know? Were you here alone?"

"No … " She clutched him to her spasmodically. "I know you were here, but we can only speak from our own points of view. Nothing like that ever happened to me. I wonder if it ever will again?"

He kissed her into silence but vocal silence only. Nature reared up and smote them and caused racing blood again to transport them into action. Gone was the frightening urgency, the tearing blasting fever of their first passion. In its place was a relative calm, ineffably sweet closeness that for all its gentleness seemed to transport them to a headier strata of appreciation. The awful impact of the earlier meeting was replaced by a quieter, more peaceful achievement that made Dariel weep softly and a lump rise to Don's throat. And she would not release him.

An hour later they ate a hearty breakfast of country sausages, scrambled eggs and crisp toast, washed down by strong hot coffee.

"On top of everything else you can cook," he said chaffingly.

Her eyes became wet. "Even the sound of your voice makes a weeper of me," she said, striving to hold her voice together. "Don, how do you do that to me? I'm no wide-eyed adolescent."

His face grew serious as he sipped his coffee. "You did the same thing to me and again that old question pops up. What now?"

"Why not more of the same? Why must something drastic always be done? After all, that's my line, you know. I'm supposed to become the possessive female, the strangling vine that soon has her man in such a state of asphyxia that he starts working late at the office and gets artificial respiration where ever he can find it."

"I think," he said with a smile of relief, "my saying that is understandable. One grows to expect it, actually becomes infected with the virus. After all, I've got no immediately visible future and what's the hurry?"

"Why not let me be your future, Don?"

His face went carefully blank. "But you just said—"

"I didn't mean it that way. If I thought marriage would spoil what we had last night I'd never marry you. I don't believe it would, but what I meant was economically. I need someone like you."

"Doesn't Abel look out for your interests?"

"He did. Not any more—understandably, I think."

"Sure. I had forgotten for a moment. What could I do?"

She laughed. "There's no hurry, remember? Let's not talk about it here. Let's never talk about anything here but you and me and what a lovely place our heaven is."

The thought sobered her suddenly. She got up to walk to a window fronting the lake, pulled the curtains and looked out where the pink sun danced on the waves. She wore a sarong sort of skirt of heayy white silk that wrapped around her waist and was held in place by a red leather belt. Above was a simple blue silk blouse that fitted loosely in all the places it could. She was barefoot and as she stood on her toes, a leg quivered, showing that it still suffered from her efforts of the night before. A ray of sunlight, lancing across the dinette, struck a leg and revealed the richness of her skin. Her hair was drawn back simply and tied with a ribbon the color of her blouse. Knowing what must be on her mind he got up and went to her. He put his arms around her from behind. Although he might have been, he was not prepared for the shock of her warm softness pressed close to him and the anatomical betrayal made a rigor flit through her muscles. Her long fingers covered his hands and twisting her neck she kissed him with a tenderness that belied the lashing passion behind it.

She sighed and faced the lake again. "I guess we're just well met. Where do you suppose this would stop, Don?"

"Another question better left to the ages. This is now."

She turned around and faced him. "That's right. Now and here." She went into his arms, her hot eager lips having lost their tenderness and become carnivorous.

The stuttering breath in her throat begged him on, on into the embrace of a white and tan goddess where all things waited in ready eagerness, impatiently then rhythmically, then with a touch of a mad haste. The keening lute in her throat announced with shrill crescendo that the portals had opened and the deluge was upon them.

They showered, dressed in bathing suits and played over the surface of the lake the rest of the morning in the big speedboat, acting like children and cutting wide swaths of foam in the blue surface of the water. At noon, feeling the deep solar warmth which their skins had gathered from the sun, they sat on the cool verandah, eating thick sandwiches and drinking beer. By common consent nothing of the past was mentioned.

"I guess we'd better get back to town," murmured Don, comfortably draining the last of his beer. "Aunt Molly might get worried."

"No one worries about me but my bankers," she said with a lonely timbre in her voice.

"That was yesterday," he replied soberly. "That's all changed now."

She bent over and rested her forehead on his forearm. "Thanks awfully," she whispered and when she raised her head his arm was wet.

He became irritated. "You know, people have treated you badly and dammit, you don't deserve it. I don't like that."

"I don't care any more—now."

He nodded. "That's right. Just remember it. You going to put your shorts outfit back on?"

She stood up. "Yes. I don't like to deplete my camp wardrobe to wear back home. After a while it all manages to wind up in the wrong place."

He sat comfortably smoking and trying to put the pieces of the last twenty four hours in some order. Then he thought of the pieces themselves and smiled. How could they be placed in order when they were not of orderly origin? They had happened; that was about all one could say.

"Don?"

"Yes?"

"Would you come here a moment, please?"

He got up and went in but he didn't see her. "Where are you?"

"In the bathroom."

He opened the bathroom door and stopped. Her hair had been swept up as it was when he first saw her, but she was entirely unclothed and without makeup, her body faintly dusted with powder. Her smile was tremulous and apologetic. "I'm sorry." Her chin trembled slightly. "I just wanted you once more."

She stood proudly in front of the big mirror that was cut to three-way reflection so he found himself staring at three luscious women, each from a different angle. And then there were three women and three men, their bodies molded as tightly as their lips.

They left the camp considerably later than they had intended, but neither voiced a protest. Don leaned back, half asleep, his mind and body so completely relaxed that speech would have been sacrilegious. Dariel drove easily, her face composed and pearly with a kind of peace attainable in only one manner. As they neared Black Point she stirred and glanced at him, her already soft expression melting further. "Don, will you come to the office tomorrow?"

"Office?" He straightened up and came back to the present. "What office?"

"Mine. I have one in the Bismark Building."

"If we get caught they'll throw you out."

"They can't. I own the place."

"Gad, a financier with an office. Sure, I'll come up. What's the deal?"

"I'll want to talk business with you. I mentioned I could use you."

"I'll be there."

"Don."

"Yeah."

"Do you have any qualms about working for a woman?"

"Nope. Not a qualm."

"I mean—like working for me. You won't feel I'm making a job for you?"

"Are you?"

"No."

"All right. I'll take your word for it. I don't think I'd care to be paid a salary for doing nothing, but I'll know pretty fast whether it's a job or not. I'm not one of these bull-headed pride boys. I'm an engineer with a degree from A. and M., but I don't have a job. I need a job and engineers of my stripe come a dime a dozen. I never liked it but it was a course to take. Besides, like a lot of kids I still unconsciously connected the term 'engineer' with a man who pulled the throttle on a locomotive. If you have a job and I can handle it I'll take it and be glad of the chance."

"See me in the morning. Shall I take you home or let you out some place?"

"Take me home. Nothing can happen to me. I'm the town's hero, remember?"

"After what happened last night and today I can laugh at them, too, but I'm no heroine. I'm just a gal who sees what it can be like. After that what is gossip?"

He leaned his head back. "Tawdry applause from small souls. Turn left."

She deposited him in front of his aunt's house, an old two story house that was not old enough to blame its pretentious turrets and gingerbread dustcatchers on tradition.

CHAPTER THREE

IT WAS Monday morning and Dariel was speaking. "When I mentioned I was loaded, Don, I wasn't kidding."

"I didn't say you were." He caressed the smooth leather of the chair with his fingertips.

"I know, but I wanted to give you some idea of the scope of it. Robert's family is dead and he naturally left everything to me. I have some acreage in Spindle-top, I have a lot of acreage in the Rio Grande Valley. I have a ranch in Mexico and some mining property."

"I'll say you're not kidding," he said with a grin. "I think I'll marry you for your money."

"You'll have to get in line. There are plenty with just that idea, believe me."

"Now that I know what you own, where do I come in?"

She toyed with a letter opener on her desk and was silent for a moment. He swept the office with his eyes for the tenth time and sniffed the air conditioning. It was a huge office with blonde maple panelling, buff leather chairs and couch, and a deep rich carpet of robin's egg blue. The desk was large and covered with a composition material that matched the chairs. There was a telephone on it, an ashtray, an intercom, two phones and a neat letter box.

"Don, this may sound silly to you, especially since you've been a flyer. I don't believe Robert is dead."

A current licked through him, bringing him to the edge of the chair. "Come over that again."

"I just don't believe it. At any rate I don't believe he died in the plane crash."

"Why?"

"Because he was too good a pilot. Didn't you ever know a pilot you thought was that good?"

He grinned. "Sure. Me! I just didn't feel I'd go out that way. I came damn near it enough times, though. Wasn't the identification good?"

"Perfect. Good enough for the insurance companies and the courts. He was very badly burned. The corpse had his build, his billfold—I didn't know a billfold was so hard to burn. There was his wedding ring, his wristwatch. Everything just like it should have been. And his plane. Still, I'm not convinced."

A spot of cold touched Don in the pit of the stomach. "Dariel, you want me to find him?"

"I want you to try. I think I'd be better satisfied if you tried and came up with nothing."

"Suppose I found him?"

The silence fell thickly and remained for some time. "You must have thought of that," he prompted somewhat harshly.

Her mouth drew in at the corners. "Yes," she almost whispered, "I've thought of that."

He crunched his hands together, the knuckles popping loudly. "Now, as the little boy said upon being accepted by the little girl, what do I do now?"

"I don't understand."

"I don't either. All of a sudden the thought of your husband coming back an Enoch Arden to look in at the window gives me the trembles."

"Because of the weekend?"

He straightened up and looked her squarely in the eyes. "What else? I didn't know you before then."

Her smile was tender. "There's no hurry, Don."

He shook his shoulders to relieve the tension which had built up. "Until you mentioned him, there was no hurry. But now, dammit, I'm scared to death."

"But you'll go?"

He massaged his hands tightly. "I'd have to go now whether I want to or not. Tell me something. When did you decide to start a search for him?"

Her eyes were serious, very deep and liquid. "When we were riding back from the lake."

"Well, I'll be damned."

"To quote you, I was there too, Don. Remember?"

His brain buzzed fitfully and to clear it he stood up and paced on the carpet. "Where was the wreck?"

"In Mexico near the silver mine, not far from a little village called Telecos."

"Who saw the body first?"

"Some Mexican farmers, I suppose. A Captain Soldarez called me about it. He's a captain of the *Rurales* in the area, a highly educated and polished gentleman. I liked him."

"What's he like?"

"Rather tall for a Mexican, sort of Hollywoodish, trim moustache, wears his uniform like a matador and I'd say is a devil with the women."

"Why, because he ogled you? Anyone would do that."

"He got his eyes full, but he was very subtle about it. No, I say so because he just looks the type. He'll be your first contact and a good man to cultivate. Know any Spanish?"

"I do all right."

"That's always a help. Can you leave soon?"

"Any time. If I stay around here the boys'll think up other inquisitions. You coming?"

"No."

"Why?"

She tapped the letter opener on a lacquered nail. "That's a hard question, Don."

"Tell me," he asked, "do you want him found?"

"You're full of hard questions today."

He grunted. "Well, at least you didn't go huffy on me."

"No, I'm not offended. Can't we just drop that angle of the matter?"

He spent more than the necessary time lighting a cigarette. "I'm in something of a turmoil, Dariel. I personally don't care a hoot about finding him. You're daddy telling a little boy to go get a switch which will be used to whip said little boy. You've no idea how hard it is to find a switch when you know you're going to get the business end of it."

"That's one reason why I'm sending you. Don, don't you want to know as badly as I do?"

He thought for a while then nodded slowly. "When you put it that way, the answer is yes. You thought this all out, didn't you?"

"I did. Both of us are being very modern about us, very casual and very careful, and yet when something shows even a possibility of coming between us, it throws us both for a loss. Are we afraid of admitting something?"

"That's one way of putting it. Do you have something concrete that you're basing this suspicion on, or is it your woman's intuition?"

"I'm not sure. What I'm afraid of is that way deep inside me there's something that would be good evidence. Something I heard or saw, maybe. I don't know, but I'm as sure as I can be that he didn't die in the crash."

"And unless he's been killed another way you feel he's alive."

"I do and if he is—" She made a graceful gesture with her hands. "Just think what that would mean."

He inhaled a quantity of smoke and let it dribble from his nose as he looked studiously at the carpet. "It would mean that he staged the disappearance or that he was a victim of a plot. A very well carried out plot. A plot that would necessitate a wide knowledge of your husband. Who's capable of pulling such a deal as that?"

"I've racked my brains. Robert did practically all his own field work. He didn't let anyone travel and inspect for him. Naturally he had his managers and secretaries and the like, but he always insisted on being there in person for inspection. He never let them know when he would arrive and in that way he caught them out on a limb plenty. He fired a lot of help and now his staff is about as good as you'll find. He never kept a man long who wasn't up to snuff."

"No one left here with him?"

"No one. He left alone and I know because I took him to the airport."

"Has be any air maps lying around?"

"Lots of them. Why?"

"I'd like to get an idea of his routes. I'll have to check them. Another thing. Is there anything to indicate that he might have disappeared voluntarily?"

She thought for a moment. "Not necessarily. He withdrew two hundred thousand dollars the day before he left but that in itself wasn't unusual, especially when he was going to Mexico. He always had a lot of deals moving down there and often took large amounts of cash."

"Any found in the wreck?"

"None. I didn't mention it at the time because I didn't think of it until I got the bank statement. I asked Captain Soldarez if any money had been found but he said only what was in the bill-fold. The luggage and everything else was a crisp."

"Did he have affairs with women?"

"Probably. It wouldn't surprise me. His taste was too good for it ever to get back to me."

"Then you wouldn't know of any woman who might have enticed him away."

"No. Nothing like that."

"Even two hundred thousand dollars isn't much for a man to elope with. Not a man who had what he had."

"Robert always said it was enough to get started on. He said he could take two hundred thousand and make a million in no time."

Don laughed ruefully. "I wish I could say that."

"When will you leave?"

He shrugged. "I'd like to see you tonight—at the lake."

Her eyes grew warm and possessive. "I'd like that, too. Shall I pick you up?"

"Right. About seven?"

"That's still daylight. Do you mind?"

"If I did you'd never know it. See you at seven."

On the way to the lake Don felt as though his universe was being torn to bits and he was the instrument of the rending as well as one of the ones to suffer. The late afternoon air was cool in their faces as the car hissed around the crooked road that bordered the lake. Late swimmers could be seen and boats skimmed the surface of the water at high speed, leaving foam and waves in their wakes.

He turned to her suddenly. "Stop the car."

She braked the car to a stop. "What's the matter?"

His face was tense and a little pale. "I want to hold you for a moment, to kiss you. Do you mind?"

"Oh, no. Oh, no." She fell into his arms and they clung to each other motivated by the same fear. Her lips were damp hot things of life that punished him to the core with their hungry sweetness and her body was a serpent that could not be still.

He released her and gazed into the depths of her eyes. "I needed that," he said huskily. "God, how I needed that."

"I did, too," she whispered. "An awful lot. And I still need you, all of you."

"You may have all I have to give, darling. Let's be moving."

She wore strap sandals and a skirt of light blue denim. Above it was a T-shirt of Navy blue which she filled with such distraction that he had stopped trying to see out of the corner of his eyes and watched her openly. The column of her neck rose from the dark jersey, strong and pure in every line, blending perfectly with jaw and head. Her ears peeked out occasionally as the wind whipped her hair aside, as pink and delicate as seashells. A sudden gust whipped through the car and blew the full skirt up, unveiling a strong tanned thigh all the way to the cobwebby bronze underthings as frail as gossamer. Without volition he leaned over and kissed the satiny surface, making her writhe with sweet anguish. Her hand fell to the back of his head and urged him gently. His teeth nibbled at the skin to such devastating effect that she almost ran the car off the road.

"Please, Don. Wait a little while. I can't stand it."

He sat erect again, but she did not pull the skirt down. The last rays of the setting sun had sent back a sunburst of riotous color that dyed the surface of her leg, making the tiny hairs stand out like the finest fur.

"I don't know how long I can stand it, either," he said, mopping his face. "And you want me to find the very man who'll break this up."

"He'll never break us up, Don—dead or alive."

"What?"

"I mean that. Robert seemed a very dashing sort who had everything. I thought I was in love with him, but I wasn't. He wanted someone to decorate his home, but he was rarely there to see the decorations. He wasn't very good at it, either. He knew business, and that was all. He didn't know women."

"Then why—"

"Because I've got to know. I can't go on wondering." Her eyes were pools of supplication, begging him to understand. "Because, you see, Don—I might want to marry you some day. I wouldn't want it to stand in the way."

"Yes. I see now, and of course, you're right. Personally, I think he's dead. You don't and you have to know."

"That's right. I have to know because I'd always be afraid."

She applied the brakes and slid the Packard under the spreading branches of a fragrant mimosa. "We're here," she said breathlessly, her long fingers tightening on the steering wheel.

"And I can safely continue my explorations." He applied his lips to the column of her throat. She emitted a low moan.

"Oh Don, Don, why can't I get epough of you?"

"This," he said harshly as he straightened up, "is madness of the purest sort. It's abnormal. No woman should put out the attraction you do. I—" He caught her to him, his teeth bruising her lips, mauling her body and striving to make it a part of him.

"Let's go in the house," he croaked.

He helped her from the car, staggering a little, and arm in arm they went up on the verandah and into the house.

She turned on the lights and tilted the blinds while he made drinks for them and set the phonograph in action again.

They danced, but their heated bodies wouldn't allow it for long. She was dead against him, her eyes closed and her senses drinking him in like a rare beverage. He picked her up and started for the bedroom, feeling the sharp points of her lacquered nails in his back and the beat of her breath on his neck. A tendril of hair tickled his nose and made a shudder course through his body. He put her down on the bed and his eyes devoured her milky tan body and the triumphant pout of her breasts. Then something snapped within her. She flung herself at him and seemed to go mad in her search for release.

Later when all was quiet she stroked his face with her fingertips and murmured in a cooing voice. "This is all ours, Don, all ours. No matter what."

"No matter what," he echoed and closed her lips with his own.

CHAPTER FOUR

THE DC-6 muttered smoothly south and below Don could see the flat richness of the Rio Grande valley and the silver thread that was the river itself. He saw it, but it failed to make much impression. He was resolutely forcing his mind into channels that had nothing to do with what he had seen at the airport when he left Black Point.

It had been early morning when they arrived at the airport, but they had had only a fifteen-minute wait before the big plane scraped its wheels, coasted up the apron, and discharged four passengers. Abel Hackett had been around smirking at a distance, a matter which Don ignored with rock-like indifference. Then Dariel had kissed Don goodbye and he had climbed aboard with two other passengers. The plane taxied down to the end of the runway, turned around and took off toward the apron. When they were airborne he glanced at the tiny terminal building. He saw Dariel in a hearty clinch with Abel. He was certain it was Abel because of the dark blue suit he wore as well as a huge gardenia that decorated his lapel. That it was Dariel he needed no evidence other than the unmistakeable figure that met his eyes.

His first reaction had been a blind scorching flame of anger, then as that passed came the familiar dull choking ache that he knew so well. Now he was concerned principally with achieving a mental vacuum through which little could pass, either memory of what had happened or what unfolded beneath the plane in the way of scenery.

Finally, completely exhausted, he went to sleep and was awakened only by the slight jar as the plane struck the runway of his first leg.

Villa Enriquez was a large city for Mexico and he knew he had a rather bumpy, decidedly hot bus trip before he reached Telecos. Still in his numb state of mind, Don took a taxi to the bus station and after a hot hour's wait boarded the bus. It was probably the worst conveyance of its kind he had ever used, but after seeing to the stowage of his effects he got aboard and sat back, not expecting to enjoy the ride.

He didn't. Dust filtered through a multitude of cracks stinging his nostrils and gritting between his teeth. He hadn't noticed anyone but Mexicans on the bus and for the most part they were silent and taciturn which was all right with him. He didn't care for their excited speech to dent the wall of sodden thoughtlessness behind which he was now securely entrenched—so he thought. One bump considerably more severe than the rest dumped a girl directly into his lap. She bounced up immediately, her smooth regular features pink with embarrassment.

"I ask your pardon, Señor," she said in a musical voice, her English quaint and accented.

He smiled. "Not at all. Maybe I saved you from a bruise."

She smiled in return, revealing teeth as white as porcelain and as even as a dental ad. She affixed her arm to a strap and looked ahead, brushing her white piqué dress with a tan, graceful hand.

He blinked and with one swift look saw that this was no ordinary girl. Don always had a weakness for the dark types, and he found that this girl was the equal, if not superior to any of the type he had ever seen. She was as slim as a reed, taller than the usual Mexican girl, her legs subtly rounded, bare and smooth as silk. Her waist he might have spanned with his hands, but the elegant swell of her breasts above lurched outward, gouging the material of her. dress into conical tents of delight. She flashed him another glance and flushed again, making him remember that he wasn't being much of a gentleman.

He sprang to his feet. "Will you accept my seat, Senorita? I would have offered it before but I hadn't noticed that you were standing."

"Oh, no sir, I couldn't take your seat."

"And why not? You've been standing for miles."

She raised her eyes to his for a moment and the shock of them made him weak in the knees. They were large, and rich velvety brown, framed in luxuriant lashes that seemed lighted by some inner fire, making luminous crescents about her eyes. The brows were thick and shone with the same fire and had never felt a tweezer. She studied him silently for a moment, and then a smile crept across her face.

"You are very kind, sir. I'll take the seat because I am very tired. I really shouldn't."

"Nuts," he said more roughly than he intended. She had thrown him off balance by her calm regard and he felt a little irritated. "I've been on a plane and I'm not at all tired."

She sat with a graceful twist of her lithe body and primly arranged her skirt around her knees.

From his greater height, Don could appreciate her even better than he had at first glance. Her head was well-shaped and her hair was a mass of stygian waves that glinted as errant rays of sun crept over and caressed it. Her neck was a column of the purest sculpture and again he was struck with the enticing regularity of her features, as delicately contrived as some costly figurine. The neck of the dress was cut low and from his height he could see the swells of her breasts as they disappeared into some gesture of restraint. A slow wave of blood swelled upward from her throat and dyed her face again. She was conscious that he was giving her a close examination. She put a hand to her throat in a nervous gesture and then took it away. The skin of her hands was as rich in color and quality as was that of her face. If she did hard work, she must spend a great deal of time on hand care, he thought. He looked away for a time until the bus stopped and the other occupant of the seat, a wizened Mexican with whiskers and no teeth, got off and left a vacancy. There was a three-man dive for the seat from the back of the bus, but Don barred their way with a big arm and said to the girl, "Would you rather sit by the window?"

She hesitated for a moment. "If I say no, you'll make me take it anyway, won't you?"

He laughed. "Of course I will."

She moved over and patted the seat. "In that case I might as well."

He ignored the black scowls of those he had blocked and sat beside her. "Since we're riding together, maybe it would be easier if we knew each other's name. I'm Don Gerdt from Black Point, Texas."

She smiled brightly. "I'm Deldee Cortez. I live in Telecos. Are you going there?"

"If I weren't I'd change my plans now." She didn't understand for a moment; then she blushed deliciously.

"You certainly turn the blood off and on," he said grinning. "I'd say you're sixteen."

"A failing of mine," she said, averting her head. "I can't help it. I'm nineteen."

"I wouldn't even try to help it. It's cute."

Her dark eyes swung around and rested with their upsetting steadiness on his. "Are all Americans as nice as you?"

Not an easy man to blush, Don felt his own face heat up with traitorous blood which he tried to laugh off, matching her own laughter that rang out like silver bells. "I'm the only one like me," he said feeling that his laugh had been as false as the ring of a lead coin.

"My father has told me about Americans. He's one himself."

"He is? I would have thought you were pure Mexican."

"I am—as such things go. My father was born in San Antonio. All of his children were too. I went to the third grade in school before we came back to Mexico.

"You speak good English, although it has an accent."

She nodded. "My father has always insisted that we use English well. We speak it at home a great deal. My mother speaks no English, but she understands it."

They chatted on as bus acquaintances will and Don began to feel a relief he had not thought possible. The pain set up by Dariel's act had dwindled considerably; Deldee was what it took to drive painful thoughts far away.

She was natural, unspoiled, without the expected feminine mystery which so many are prone to cultivate. Her conversation was free and, except for her proclivity for blushing, which he enjoyed, she was in every way a charming girl and excellent company.

"Where will you stay in Telecos?" she asked.

He shrugged. "I suppose there'll be some sort of hotel."

"There is—of a sort. You won't like it. It has roaches."

"Is it dirty?"

She lifted her shoulders slightly. "Not too bad, but I wouldn't like to have to stay there. It has roaches."

"Where else is there to stay?"

"It is the only hotel. Señor Don, would you think it forward if I asked you to stay with us?"

"Oh, come now, Deldee. I couldn't impose on your family like that."

She was eager. "It would be no imposition, really. We have quite a large house."

"But what would your mother and father think of you inviting a total stranger to your house."

Her eyes were enticing. "You were very nice to me when you didn't have to be. We have talked a long time and now we're not strangers; we're friends. You have made no improper suggestions to me and I can tell you come from a nice family. That's all Father would want to know."

He laughed with real amusement. "No. I couldn't do that Deldee, really. If your family took in boarders I might"

"They've talked about it a lot," she said breathlessly. "We have lots of room and they've talked many times of having boarders if they could have nice people."

He squared around and faced her. "Tell me, why exactly do you want me to go to your house? You never saw me before today. This invitation, while certainly appreciated, is a little odd."

"Because I know you won't like the hotel. They have rooms *with*."

He didn't catch the significance of her last words and stared thoughtfully at the dusty floor of the bus for a while. "Well, I'll go to the hotel and you can ask your father. If he says it's all right, then I'll move out of the hotel. Tell him I'm on an expense account and can pay him well."

This condition seemed to satisfy her and their conversation turned to other things.

The bus was now laboring up a winding road that seemed to lead to a notch in the mountains ahead. Deldee noticed him looking, and said, "Over the pass is Telecos. About twenty more miles."

He mopped his face and looked at the streaks of grime it left on his handkerchief. "I'll be glad. This has been a gritty ride."

"I'll be glad, too," she agreed fervently. "I hate to be dirty and on this ride you can't help it."

"Do you make the trip often?"

"No. I go to Villa Enriquez once or twice a year to try to get a job as a stenographer, but I never get the job. Too much else besides typing and shorthand."

"Like what?"

She flushed again. "Fat greasy men who want to paw me and always speak of late hours, taking me to dinner, and things like that."

"And that you don't like?"

"I don't like it." She tossed her thick soft hair and sighed. "There's nothing in Telecos."

"How big is it?"

"Very small. Maybe a thousand people. There is some mining, although it has almost played out. But the valley is rich and raises much food. Trucks come and haul it away. We have some rain and good water."

They reached the top of the pass and spread below them was a sere rocky valley that didn't look rich and productive to Don. But at last he could make out the strip of green at the far end, and the metallic shimmer of the small river that wound snake-like across the horizon.

Her face was alight as she looked and the other passengers seemed to come to life. Soft liquid Spanish could be heard and there was a general movement of anticipation. Downhill the going was rougher because the speed was greater; they had to hold on to avoid getting thrown off the seat. Speech was difficult until they reached the floor of the valley and then they were very close to the town. Green growing things could be seen now. Excellent vegetable patches, waving corn, fat grazing cattle and numerous fruit orchards. The smell of the air was cooler and sweet.

"You turned this trip from a drudge into a delight, Deldee. Thanks a lot."

"You were nice to me," she said simply, "when you didn't have to be. Father says that is the American way. If I made the ride pleasant, then I'm glad."

"I never met a girl quite like you," he said, feeling that he was -uttering an understatement.

Her look was puzzled. "I'm just a girl."

"No, you're not just a girl. You're a very beautiful girl. A girl with intelligence and understanding."

She nodded slightly. "I think I have a good brain. But you mustn't say I'm beautiful."

"Why not? You are beautiful."

Her eyes seemed to grow darker as they met his. "Only lovers say those things, Señor."

"Oh, come off it," he laughed. "I merely made a statement of fact. I could look at your picture and say the same thing."

"You've told that to many girls?"

"No, as a matter of fact, I haven't. Not the way I told you. I wasn't trying to be forward or to flirt."

"Yes, I know that. You said it as though you meant it."

"Of course, I meant it. It's nothing to be upset about."

"No, I suppose not, but—" Her eyes suddenly filled with tears. "No one ever told me that before."

He touched her hand, cut to the quick. "No one ever told you that?"

She moved her hand gently away. "No. No one who meant it and wasn't trying to—" She turned her head and looked out across the landscape.

Don's heart ached fiercely for a moment, then hardened against the impact of her, hardened as he had trained it to do whenever emotion threatened to destroy his equilibrium.

"That," he said softly, "is a shame. Don't you have boy friends?"

She shrugged and took some time answering, still looking out of the window. "Wait till you see Telecos. The better families are stuck up and the others are impossible." With a jerk she swung around and faced him. "Maybe I did have a reason for wanting you to stay at my house. Is that wrong?"

"Of course not." Then his tongue stuck and words would not come for a while. "Not wrong Deldee, but—" He stopped again and frowned at her, thinking hard. Here was a girl with whom it would not do to trifle. She was sensitive and very tender. She would hurt easily.

"You needn't say it," she said with a sob. "I'm forward and just the sort to be a stenographer for those men I mentioned."

"Nothing of the sort," he said crossly. "You're punishing yourself unnecessarily."

"You're being kind again." She took a deep breath and her breasts raked the soft material of her dress in a manner that made his skin tighten. "Please. Can you understand that I'm a grown girl who has never known the sweetness of a man's kiss, who has never sat in the moonlight with my head on his shoulder and listened to him whisper things in my ear? I have never known love, except to know that within my breast is a quantity of it that no man has ever shared. You're nice, you're a kind man and handsome in a rough craggy sort of way. I like the way your hair is combed, I like the shape of your head, I like the little wrinkles at the corners of your eyes, I like that little twist at the right corner of your mouth. Is it hard to understand that I would want to see you more? Am I bad because I tried?"

"None of those things are true, Deldee," he said gently, "and I do understand. But I couldn't stay at your house unless your father were willing. There's just one more thing. Don't feel that way about what you've done. I said you're beautiful and I say it again." He sighed and squeezed her shoulder. "I hope your father gives his consent. If it is true that you wish to see more of me, it is no less true that I'd like to see you too. I think you're excellent company and you're certainly a charming person."

Her eyes seemed bottomless as she wet her lips and took a shuddering breath. "You are very kind. I've said that before. I never met anyone like you. You said that about me. We will get off the bus soon. I will send my little brother tomorrow with a note."

I'll be waiting."

CHAPTER FIVE

T HE TOWN was built on either side of the river and had two stone bridges connecting the two main streets. The bridges suggested wealthier days; they were huge structures that would have withstood any load and seemed very old.

Adobe buildings were scattered without order up and down the gorge that contained the river. They were whitewashed and their red tile roofs were bright in the late afternoon sun. The church was large with round stone dome in place of a steeple and occupied the central spot, surrounded by what he took to be convent buildings and other structures connected with the church.

The Hotel Europa was a sprawling, many-winged, two-storied, stuccoed affair, that meandered aimlessly over a large plot of ground. Whatever might have been the short comings of the hotel, the grounds were impeccable. Someone with an eye for arrangement and a green thumb had worked long and hard to produce the flowerbeds, shade trees and green closely clipped sward. It looked cool and inviting, but at the moment Don was anxious for a bath.

A dapper little man stood behind the desk and bowed deeply. "Welcome, Señor," he said in bad English, "to our humble diggings. The finest has been reserved for you."

Don stared at him. "By whom?"

"The excellent Captain Soldarez came in person and arranged it."

"You mean Soldarez of the local *rurales?*"

"No less, sir. Now, the room can be had both with or without as they do in the *Estados Unidos.*"

Don blinked and recalled what Deldee had said, still not getting the meaning. "With or without what?"

It was the clerk's turn to blink. "Why, women of course." He lowered his voice. "It is, of course, not really the hotel's responsibility. That I have taken upon myself, having served many American men and even women in like manner. I understand it is quite the expected thing in your country."

Don laughed. "Well, not too common any more. The war, you know."

"Ah, yes—the war. Many things have changed."

"I didn't get what you meant for a while. Where could I find Captain Soldarez?"

"He is expecting you and he asked that I extend his felicitations and invitation to dinner. He honors our table quite often."

"Here?"

"Sí—I mean, yes. He mentioned the hour of seven."

"I'll go up now and bathe some of Mexico off me and shave. That'll make it about time."

"By all means. You will find that your room possesses an excellent shower."

The shower was good and the water better. It was bone-aching cold and nothing could have suited Don better. Moreover, a sign said in lurid red letters, THIS WATER IS EXCELLENT FOR THE DRINKING.

He tried it and found it so. It had none of the astringent bite of the brackish stuff which served Black Point. It was not usual Mexican water, but it was good.

He shaved and found it quite soft, another point in its favor. After his shave and bath he dressed in cool black and white cord with shoes to match and ran a comb through his unruly hair.

Feeling considerably improved both in body and appearance, he walked down the cool tiled corridor to the stairs and descended.

Leaning as lightly as a gymnast against the desk in casual conversation with the clerk was the most improbably smooth article in the way of a militarily dressed man Don had ever seen. His uniform, tailored with staggering perfection, was of no country in the world, resembling that of Mexico only by the metal ornaments which adorned it; these were polished to a blinding brilliance. And the man was no less extravagant than the uniform. He stood easily six feet two, and probably weighed one hundred eighty or ninety. It was hard to tell because of the unique perfection of his build. The tremendous shoulders tapered delicately downward into a broad chest which in turn tapered into an almost waspish waist and thin fleshless hips. His legs, as revealed through the material of the uniform, were strong and straight. Here was masculine symmetry at its best.

As Don approached the dream straightened up, clicked his heels gently, and bowed from the waist.

"Have I the honor of addressing Señor Don Gerdt?"

Don, who had taken an instant dislike to Soldarez, felt it melting away promptly before the power of the man's personality.

"Such as it is, you have it. You're Captain Soldarez?"

"Such is my wretched title. You seem to have made the trip in good order."

The captain's grip was like a vise, a matter which evaporated the rest of Don's resentment.

"Very good except for some sore spots gathered on the bus."

"Wretched conveyance," said Soldarez, with a grimace. "My—er, heart aches for you. Would you consider it an affront if I suggested a drink before dinner?"

"I'd consider it an affront if you didn't. Lead the way."

With a bow the soldierly figure stepped lithely away, ramrod straight and as light as a feather. His skin, Don noticed, might have rivalled Deldee's for purity of color and smoothness. Only by the closest examination could the necessity for shaving be seen, except for the piratical moustache which was so perfect it seemed to have been stenciled on. His lips were thin but not severe, having a curiously soft and relaxed, almost feminine, appearance.

"Ah, here we are. Shall we take a table or stand at the bar?"

"In spite of miles of sitting, the prospect of standing appalls me. If it's soft, I'll sit."

They sat in a corner half shaded from the rest of the tiled bar by a potted palm. The bar was dark and cool, with a heavy oak beamed ceiling and dark wood panelling running three feet up from the floor where white stucco took over and extended to the ceiling. The bar itself was massive mahogany darkened by the ages until it looked blackened.

"I can recommend to you a variety of American, French, Mexican and Canadian whiskies as well as the best scotch. What will it be?"

"Make it American bourbon, a triple with a little water and ice."

A waiter, who must have been hiding behind the palm ducked around, took the order and vanished.

"I see you're treated almost as royalty around here. How do you do it?"

Soldarez grinned, flashing brilliant white teeth against the darkly tanned skin of his face. "It's a gift. By the way, Mrs. Caraway phoned and asked me to watch out for you."

Don's face went grim. "Yes, I'm working for her."

Soldarez lifted a questioning eyebrow, but did not frame the query in words. The drinks came, and they toasted each other silently.

"Room satisfactory?"

"Oh, sure. Better than I had hoped. The water's good."

"Best water in Mexico and lots of it. We're fortunate here."

Don put his drink down and sat back. "Tell me, my improbable friend, what are you doing here?"

Both the swallow-winged eyebrows went up, then came down as the Captain laughed. "What's wrong with me being here?"

"Nothing, except everything. You're too smooth, too handsome, too assured, too well spoken, too well dressed, and I think as I know you better I can elaborate on these points."

Soldarez lit a long black cigarette and inhaled with relish. "It would take some time to answer your question categorically, but enough for now to say that I like it here."

"I venture to say that you're a flyer."

Soldarez's face went blank. "What made you think that?"

"A number of things. Were or are you?"

"Were and are. I flew with the British during the last go. I was shot down three times. Once in the channel. Twice I escaped from *Stalag-Luft* Fifteen."

Don's eyes narrowed. "You wouldn't have happened to have chosen the name Felipe Mendoza for that last go, would you?"

Again came the magnetic grin. "I see my poor efforts did not go unnoticed."

"Not by a lot. And here you are, a dressed-up constable."

"By choice, I assure you. You see—pardon the early familiarity, Mr. Gerdt, but may I use your first name?"

"By all means. Been meaning to ask you the same thing."

"You may call me Phil. Felipe was the only real part of my name that I used with the British. I was afraid my country or my parents might object."

"You call me Don. How many Germans did you bring down?"

"Seventeen, I think the official score was. Fun. I also shot down a Bussian by mistake. Now I wonder if my enthusiasm wasn't really a kind of prescience."

"I know what you mean. I dropped several Reds myself in Korea. Tell me, do you know a family here name of Cortez?"

"Ah, yes. Old family. Descended from the original, no doubt."

"Horse feathers. That's too far to count."

Phil laughed. "Yes, isn't it? They are a really good family. The father is *alcalde* of our fair city."

"Do you know Deldee?"

"Very well. Did you meet her?"

"I think she's one of the most beautiful women I ever saw."

"Without a doubt. And quite Americanized as are a number of families here. This is a favorite spot for people in comfortable circumstances to come and live their last days. It's a quiet, healthy climate, and few tourists. Tourists help support the country, but are a pain in the neck."

"I should imagine. Phil, you nosed about when Caraway crashed. What did you find?"

"The back of an axe couldn't be blunter than that. Don't you know you're supposed to lead up to it by degrees."

"That's not my way."

"Mine either, but I use it for atmosphere. Yes, I examined the wreck."

"What did you find?"

The captain leaned back, blew a smoke ring and sent another through it as it widened. "I have thought several things."

"Like what?"

"Like why a man would go to such trouble to appear to have died and leave a fortune untouched."

"Maybe he got bored with money."

"I'm afraid you were not well acquainted with Señor Caraway. I was. There may be an explanation."

"Then you think he's still alive?"

Soldarez shrugged. "Unless he slipped on a banana peel and broke his neck."

"Dariel seems to think likewise. What do you know about it?"

"Very little, really. I'm not exactly a fool, however. There were any number -of things wrong that I did not then mention. I let the law take its appointed blundering course and made routine the order of the day."

Don, thrilled by something he could not identify, leaned forward and said slowly, "How very curious."

Phil blinked. "I beg your pardon?"

"Let's not start out being evasive. You discover a body and know that some effort has been made to make it appear that of another man. You're there in an official capacity, yet you let routine rule the investigation when you might have made yourself internationally famous."

Phil's rich laughter was sincere. "I fear you're learning me faster than I am you. Well, here's what I found. The blood, such as there was of it, showed a cadaver had been used that was just short of decomposition. The teeth that nearly always help identification were strangely absent. Had they been left they couldn't have helped because the face and head were almost completely ruined by the fire, so the extra effort there exposed the deal."

"That's all well and good, but it doesn't explain your lack of push."

"That is the one thing I cannot reveal at this time. Would you be temporarily satisfied if I said I considered it necessary?"

"Certainly—temporarily."

Suddenly the captain's face seemed to grow hard and triangular, his Indian heritage asserting itself and his eyes became bits of opaque slag. "Señor Gerdt, there is another matter for which I must beg your forbearance. Do not begin any search for Señor Caraway. Not immediately."

Don felt as though some giant hand had gripped him and sat him forty feet back. Soldarez was facing him as solid and implacable as a teak carving, his easy good humor gone, his frame seeming to tighten and ready itself for a spring.

Don sat speechless and gazed at the wooden visage before him for some time. As he did, it gradually relaxed into its former affability. "I regret that I should have to deliver an ultimatum,

Don, but I think it'll save us both temper and time. I'm sorry I can't tell you now what my reasons are. There are things about you that I shall have to learn both from investigation and observation. I must know you. Actually, you have no real knowledge of why you're here, do you?"

Don relaxed and let a sigh seep between his teeth. "Putting it that way makes me think of a lot of things. I'm here to find a dead husband."

"Why? She had the money and if you brought him back he'd be in the driver's seat again. What does she want to find him for?"

Don thought for a moment then said, "We might get married and we wouldn't want him cropping up at the wrong time."

"Do you really believe that she'd marry you?"

"It happens. Why not?"

Phil wrung his hands with one quick motion cracking the joints of his fingers cruelly. "I'm a very perceptive person. At the first mention of her name a spasm of pain, which fools mistake for hate, went over your face. Your answer was short and not quite rude."

Don's face performed again. "You have me there. I've been through three bruising battles with women and lost all three times. It hasn't hardened me; it has made me sensitive."

"That's good. Finish your drink and we'll go into the dining room. We can eat and talk."

The dining room was dim and cool with warm pastel stuccoed walls and slowly revolving ceiling fans. It was larger than Don had expected. White-clad waiters flitted nimbly about and Soldarez beckoned to one. "Hungry?" he asked Don.

"Ravenous. What's on the bill?"

"I'd suggest the sirloin or the roast beef unless you prefer fowl. We have pheasant, guinea hen, or chicken. The fish I don't recommend."

"I'll take the roast beef."

The waiter left and the captain made a steeple of his fingers and frowned at it. "I make bold to suggest that the elegant Mrs. Caraway is paying you a fabulous price for this job."

"Certainly. She has plenty."

"And yet those who have plenty invariably want more. It would have been cheaper to marry you outright, since his death has been legally certified. Had he shown up, matters might have been arranged to satisfy both parties, especially since her legal position is sound."

Don nodded and tasted the cold red wine the waiter had brought. "She said she didn't love him and would divorce him if I were successful."

Phil nodded. "And in spite of that she is sparing no expense for you to come down here and poke about."

"Well, it does seem a little odd when dissected."

"I venture further that you accepted in a very different state of mind than you now find yourself. You do not impress me as a man smitten with love."

"It happened as the plane took off. I can't imagine what she was thinking of—no matter how she felt."

"Planes are not trains or busses. People forget that sometimes. Ah! Pardon me a moment while I see if I can improve our masculine company a bit."

He skirted tables with the grace of a dancer and approached a woman who was standing in the door of the dining room. She was clad in a dress of some white synthetic material which a tailor of genius had kissed elegantly. It was strapless, but on no account could it have been considered precariously supported. Her breasts, while not large, were assertive and thorn sharp at the tips, the bases widening richly and firmly. Her hair was ash blonde and Don would have bet her eyes were blue. His guess was a good one—they were blue. A childish blue, wide and too naive to be trusted.

"Miss Carol Norman, it is my pleasure to present Señor Donald Gerdt of Texas."

"Please allow me to share some of your pleasure, Phil. I'm happy at this moment, Don." Her smile revealed small white teeth as even as the captain's. Her salutation, while joking, had a smoothness that spoke of Continental experience.

"Let's split the pleasure three ways, as we say in America." Don stood and bowed.

"If you are faced with the tragedy of dining alone," said Phil easily, "pray accept our company and prevent a similar tragedy at this table."

"I couldn't refuse an invitation like that," she said, dimpling, and allowed him to seat her.

The dinner proceeded, lit by flashes of scintillant repartee between Soldarez and Carol Norman. Don felt an undercurrent sweeping through the occasion and sat in silence for the most part. Carol was lovely; there could be no denying that. But he sensed a falseness about her which Phil seemed determined to draw out and succeeded nobly.

After the dessert she excused herself and disappeared, her hips trim and sufficient, swaying just short of positive provocation.

"And who is the mysterious Norman?"

"A Dresden figurine, but maybe a little too solidly constructed for that. Either she is the world's best actor or a courtesan that might have made Mohammed drown the rest of his wives. A mystery, all right. No apparent objective here, no obvious means of support, and yet with plenty of money to spend."

"I gather that you've lost no time."

"Time is the one indispensable commodity. As much as the prospect appalls me, I shall one day be old. She's clever, that one."

"But not clever enough?"

"Precisely. I know her three days and one night after looking over the offerings indigenous to the Plaza I wend my way to my modest diggin's and there she sits. She didn't sit long and I must say she was a delicious viand of variety. Now I have only to beckon."

"She got around to questioning you yet?"

"Very cleverly. She slugged my drinks, got me into one of my happy states of inebriation and asked me to tell her the story of my life. I was tempted to imagine some bit of fiction but she might have caught on. I told her everything—except what she wanted to know."

"What was that?"

"She cleverly refrained from telling me. If I don't skid on the curves—unintentional pirn—I may discover it. She was interested in my flying career."

"Maybe you shot down Stalin's son and she's an advance echelon of the MVD."

Phil shrugged. "Before I run the risk of shocking you again, what is your attitude toward women?"

"Oh, the usual. Not too different from yours I shouldn't think. I'm no celibate, reserve certain prerogatives of choice, and watch undergrown emotions carefully. Why do you ask?"

The captain's face went blank again. "I had several reasons. You see, womanhood is probably the greatest boon with which the gods have endowed us. I love them, all of them, the lovely ones, I mean. I play upon them and make wonderful music. I'm sickened by tragedy and I despise careless men whose personal pleasure is all they think of. I'm especially anxious that nothing of the nature of a tragedy should strike Deldee Cortez."

"Is your interest too personal to discuss?"

"She is not among my lovelies," he said with a short laugh, "simply because one does not attempt such with one's cousin. However, in all honesty I've often gnashed my teeth at the ones who set up such a code. She and Thereze and Esta are apples of my eye. Thereze is intractable, as explosive as a volcano and twice as unpredictable. Don Ramon, her father, says she grew up in the quiet of his family much after the fashion of a volcano raising its head in the middle of a peon's com field. Esta is too quiet to understand and is habitually addicted to nocturnal ramblings. This could be in search of stars and hours of artistic somnambulism. It could be something else as well. Whatever it is she has observed the sharpest care and has never been discovered. Don Ramon, with true American philosophy, lets them do as they please and hopes for the best. So far nothing has happened to cause him any lost sleep. Thereze is less careful and was caught by me with the stable boy, a slim stripling of a lad who seemed to know what he was about, so I left them undisturbed, although I cannot claim that I myself was undisturbed."

"You've mentioned them all in detail except Deldee. What about her?"

"Deldee is a great lady. Maybe under the right sort of tutelage she might become a volcano herself, but so far she has eschewed the company of such males as the valley affords. She runs deep, whereas Esta only gives that appearance the better to cloak her true self. Deldee is truly fine. A person of considerable soul, if I may use a much beaten term. I couldn't see myself becoming overly concerned about Thereze and Esta purely from the uselessness of it. But Deldee is another thing entirely."

"She's in danger, in a manner of speaking, Phil. She gets bowled over by routine kindnesses, overwhelmed at flat uninspired compliments, and she's convinced that nothing will happen to her love life in the valley."

"And who can argue with her?"

"Be that as it may, I don't think I'll accept her invitation to put up at her house even if her father doesn't object."

"On the contrary, I'd accept in a flash."

"Maybe you didn't hear me. I'm not a man of stone and your description of her might have been my own. I told you I have certain principles."

"Is one of them ducking something that might prove the best thing that ever happened to you?"

"Let's talk about something else."

"Very well, but I'd think well before I refused to be gifted with such a place to live. You'll be here for some time."

"How long?"

"That would be hard to say. Señora Caraway knows about it because I told her."

"How much?"

"Only that I wouldn't be able to allow you much freedom to pursue a search until the time was ripe. She understands and was quite agreeable. I even noted that she was too agreeable."

"What do you make of that?"

Phil shrugged dramatically. "What can one make of such things when one knows nothing?"

"You know something."

"Agreed, but not nearly enough. I shall have to council patience. One more thing—do I have your word of honor as a gentleman that you will not search or cause a search to be made for Señor Caraway or even ask questions about him?"

"You have it. And I hear myself promise that with considerable wonder. I don't know why I'm doing it."

"Without any knowledge of the reason for my request you pay me the supreme compliment of being intelligent enough to know what I'm doing." A grin lit his face, a satanic distillate. "I know some others who would feel considerably less confident if they knew what I know and knew of my own confidence."

"I wish I knew."

"It is possible that you will. The better I know you the more certain I am. Shall we hence to a cabaret where I am acquainted and commence where we left off before dinner?"

"I see I can depend on you to make timely and proper suggestions."

"I flatter myself. There are also any number of amoral companions to be had should your fancy be taken by our hayseed women."

"Those I've seen gives your descriptions the lie. I'd say you're overloaded."

"We are, and underloaded with men. It makes for a delightful situation all around, from the male point of view anyway."

"I find little of the much chronicled Mexican stiffness of social codes here. Why?"

"Who can say? There is little of the true Mexican moral outlook here. Several good families returned here from the States with North American perspectives, except that they chose to come here rather than go to Florida which many retired Americans prefer. There are, of course, some here who view the freedom of the sexes with a jaundiced eye, but these people-are about the same the world over—always present in any society."

The cabaret was considerably larger than Don had expected, built low and rambling with the ubiquitous tile roof and floor, the outside whitewashed and clean. There was a long bar against one wall with a scattering of tables and an open space for dancing between it and a bandstand which was raised somewhat from the rest of the floor. Already patrons were numerous, but all made way with respect and smiles for the captain.

For the first time in months Don really relaxed and his liquor went down with a song of joy.

Sometime between midnight and dawn Phil piloted him to the hotel without a pain in the world or a worry.

"Say, whatta 'bout a car, Phil ol' boy? Reckon I could rent one?"

"We'll see. There's always *mañana,* you know."

"Soon enough for me," sang Don as he strode into the hotel lobby, feeling transcendental and unconquerable.

The clerk, who it seemed was on duty both day and night, hissed at him. "Señor, what about *with?*"

"Bernardino," said Don grandly with a sweep of his hand, *"with*—some other time, possibly. At the moment the attractions of Morpheus are greater." Then he waltzed on up the stairs and out of sight.

"Who," snapped the clerk to the janitor, a blasé youngster of fourteen, as he plied a wet mop on the tiles, "is this woman Morph—whatever he said—and how did he know my name?"

"Ask God," said Porfirio with spurious piety.

"I'm asking you, *cabron* and if you've been sneaking around behind my back trying to ruin my business, I'll-"

Porfirio delved into the recesses of his voluminous shirt and emerged with a knife that looked dangerous enough to be arrested. He struck the flat of the blade on his hard palm and tucked it out of sight in his shirt again. "I think," he said, "that the weather will change."

"It will," said the clerk ominously. "I can promise it." But his statement was strangely lacking in force.

CHAPTER SIX

D ON WAS half undressed and thinking only of the chill of the shower when he realized that he was not alone in the room. He stiffened, then let his eyes wander around until he picked out the form of a girl hidden in the shadow of the huge cabinet where he had hung his clothes.

Seeing no reason for fright, he pursued his affable impulses and grinned. "Hello!"

She walked out of the shadow toward him, her ripe hips undulating with such shocking seductiveness that he felt as though he had touched a hot wire.

She stopped a few feet away and smiled slowly, her teeth white and clean in the dim light of the overhead bulb. She was a big girl and hefty in every department. He could see that she was proud of the magnificent cliffs of her breasts as they staggered about in her red blouse with upsetting effect.

"Señor Don."

"That's me. But who are you?"

"I am Thereze Cortez."

Without intending to, he took a step backward. She seemed to blaze with a primordial hunger. It shone from the big dusky eyes, the satin smooth skin—from the whole attitude so unmistakable in intent that he felt a cool sweat break out on his brow. Her skirt was printed cotton, advertising the full straight contours of her thighs—especially when she walked.

"This is not an hour," he pointed out, "at which ladies visit gentlemen in their rooms."

She smiled wider, dimples pitting her cheeks. "I know that. I don't like a lot of women around when I visit."

He swallowed hard and managed to get the next question out. "Why did you come? Uh, did you bring a note?"

She shook her head, her red black hair dancing and glistening under the mean light. "No, I have no note. Pepé will bring it in the morning. I came to see you."

She stepped forward and stopped so close to him that he could catch the faint impression of heat from her thinly clad body and the mild call of some flowery perfume.

The pounding beat of his heart and the feeling of soaring eagerness with which he was infected made him react as she had known he would. He returned her bold gaze and allowed it to examine her, detail by detail, from her slim ankles past the luxuriant swellings of her legs upward to her narrow waist to the bountiful assertions of her breasts. Then he looked in her eyes, and her reaction made her lick her lips slowly. In the light they seemed as smooth as cream, damp and faintly tremulous as though actually feeling the brutal pressure of his own.

The dimples came into view again as she smiled, a smile of worldly understanding, of a woman sure of her attraction and certain of its inevitable results.

"You think I'm good to look at, Señor?"

"Much better than I had dreamed," he said with husky sincerity.

"Then you've dreamed

"I've heard of you," he replied guardedly.

She stepped closer until he could feel the sharp firm prod of her breasts against his chest, the shock dimming his vision and filling his arteries with furiously charging blood.

"I'm much better to hold than to look at."

His arms went out and her own went around his neck and a throaty little gurgle came from her throat as their lips met. She fitted him like soft clay from lips to ankles but no clay ever radiated such heat or produced such intimate little movements. She broke away from him and stepped back, putting her hands to the neck of her low cut blouse and pulling slowly. Snaps made little protesting noises as they gave way to the pressure and slowly she pulled the blouse down, turning from him so that when at last it fell from her round arms to the floor all he could see was a broad back of flawless olive skin, trenched deeply and a-ripple with muscle that was not corded and hard, but softly rounded, superbly conditioned like that of a cat. She looked over a shoulder and smiled, then like a flash she turned and leaped into his embrace again, her breasts crushed against his chest with such delightful pressure that they seemed like twin arcs of unendurable sensation.

A groan almost forced itself from his throat, but her lips denied it exit. Her back, like a plain of soft satiny wonder, came under the groping caress of his hands, accelerating avidity which needed none. A guttural sound of raving hunger came from her depths. His hands slid beneath the elastic waistband of the skirt. She caught him by the wrists and with a sudden motion stood apart from him, her lips parted, her eyes smoking wells of the ecstasy to come; then slowly she came to him again, lifted her lips to his gently, and murmured. *"Querido mio, querido mio."*

The next morning Don woke feeling that he had been the victim of a peculiarly attractive dream. For a long time he lay there savoring the details of it and it was not until he tried to stand and went weakly to his knees that he realized it had been no dream. He showered and while he shaved he counted seven bloodshot spots where she had attacked him with her teeth.

He felt a twinge of something like remorse, then grinned. What the hell! If this was going to turn out just a vacation, why not make a good one of it.

He had hardly seated himself for breakfast when the dazzling Soldarez swept into the dining room, swinging a rawhide swagger stick, his cap at an angle which was effective but might have been frowned upon by most military men.

"Ah, there you are. May I suggest guinea eggs, three of them, coddled in cream with a dash of cheyenne sauce. Avast the grimace there, I didn't say chili. Quite a potent aphrodisiac. By the by, old fruit, you look as if you could use some about now. Surely you didn't duck out on the town after I so tenderly escorted you home?"

Don grinned peacefully. "No, the town came in on me. Why didn't you tell me I might expect to find a girl in my room which might have just escaped from some pasha's pipe dream?"

The swallow-wing eyebrows shot up. "Tell me more! I was the victim once of Bernardino's impossible taste in blondes. Surely this houri was not of his doing."

"No. He tried to stop me with a proposition as I went through the lobby, but I waved him off and left him cursing the janitor. For what I don't know."

"Small matter. But about this girl—what was she like?" "I'm afraid you might be offended."

"Me? Offended at love? Even such clandestine love as creeps into hotel rooms at odd hours? You do me sore injustice."

"Well, she had black hair with red overtones, sunstruck, I'd say."

"The hair or the girl? You need say no more. It was the competent Thereze. Doubtless Deldee went home full of enthusiasm about the nice American she met. I've known Thereze to become active on less provocation than that." He leaned forward, his satanic grin at full mast. "Tell me, was she—well, all right?"

"She was Paracutin in full eruption."

Phil nodded happily and gave the order to the waiter. "There must have been some lusty blooded Casanova on our family tree. Don Ramon must know that a girl like Thereze can't stay home and knit, but if the knowledge causes him any worry he doesn't show it. He's a placid old bloke."

"But look here. Suppose I go there to board? What'll I do about her?"

The grin returned. "Play her against Esta. Look, fella, what do you want for the price of a room?"

Don's flush was instantaneous. "That was a dark treacherous blow, Phil."

"I abound with them," was the retort as he ladled sugar into the cup of steaming fragrant coffee that the waiter put before him. "I have hopes for you," he continued, sipping the coffee fastidiously.

"In what way?"

"In a way you least expect and if you think I'm about to be offended because you bedded my cousin, I might point out that I should, according to family ties, be infuriated. But I realize that if you took the plenteous Thereze to love she probably had more to do with it than you. Furthermore, I can promise that she will not become the usual violated maiden and make your waking hours harrowing and your nights uneasy. She is a sensuous dream, existing for the purpose of wringing from her consciousness every possible titilatipn. She is without serious designs. Oddly enough she has rather topping taste. She's not one who will lay in wait for just any mestizo that happens to pass. You are new, well favored and most likely clean. Mexico is not noted for its cleanliness, but in this valley it is a local fetish."

"Yes, I noticed no roaches in my room although Deldee predicted I would."

"Deldee was speaking under the pressure of bias, a bias one can understand." The grin flared again. "What an enviable position you find yourself in without even asking."

"I'm seriously considering kicking your shins, Phil."

The other laughed. "By the way, I heard from Dariel this morning."

"So early? I didn't think she got up this early."

"She is concerned over your welfare and the progress of the investigation."

"Which you told her previously had been shut off."

"Of course, but after all she is a woman." He chuckled. "And I might add a wholly delightful woman."

"I was waiting for you to add that. I thought so, too."

"No need to become incensed. I didn't know you when I knew her."

"Not incensed. Just griped that I could have been roped in so easily."

"Come now. If you hadn't peeked and seen, would you have resisted Thereze?"

Don laughed. "Probably not." And for some reason he did not feel so intensely his resentment against Dariel. The breakfast came and they devoted their attention to its delicate attractions.

As they walked out on the terrace a well preserved 1940 Ford purred up and a slim lad got out, bearing an envelope.

"Comes the estimable Pepé with summons doubtlessly arranged by Deldee. Good morning, Pepé."

"Good morning, sir," said Pepé with a snappy salute.

"Pepé, you insufferably polite young hellion, allow me to present Mr. Donald Gerdt."

"It is a pleasure, sir," said Pepé, bowing from the waist.

"The pleasure is all mine," said Don, grinning. "I insist."

"You, sir," said Pepé with his eyes lowered respectfully, "haven't had the advantage of seeing me through a young woman's eyes."

Phil said, laughing, "That is an advantage. Should we hear of you from some woman it would assuredly be harmful."

"I bear a note, sir, from my father," said Pepé, tendering the envelope.

Don accepted it and opened it to read:

Sir, having endured the blandishments of my daughter Deldee—whom I gather you met and befriended on

the bus yesterday—until endurance seems less preferable than capitulation, I hereby implore that you share
our modest home until such time as your business takes
you from our village. She has assured me that you are a
man of the highest integrity and honor and I feel that my
house would be honored by your presence. In all things
your obedient servant,

Arturo Carlos Ramon Cortéz y Cordoba

Don sighed as he folded the letter slowly. "You may tell your
father that I will come as soon as I can hire a car to bring my
baggage."

"I was instructed to perform that duty, sir," said Pepé, whose
eyes held an adoration which Don found hard to explain.

"Very well, I shall have them brought out." He turned to the
grinning Soldarez. "I'm a man of honor and integrity, you grinning imp. I am going to change my lodgings and stay with Don
Ramon."

"I thought you would. I envy you. Shall I send you a man
with a car?"

"That duty also I shall be happy to perform," said Pepé hastily.

"But your father might need his car," protested Don.

"It is not his, but mine," said Pepé, proudly. I made it from
three other cars that were worn out."

"Pepé," put in Phil laughing, "is a man of talents, not solely
confined to automobiles either, as I think you will discover."
He spoke to Pepé in Spanish, which Don understood perfectly.
"Little man, guard your actions while chauffeuring this guest.
Remember my instructions."

"They are remembered," answered Pepé.

The Cortez home was almost hidden from the winding
stone-surfaced road by mimosas, tamarinds plams and banana
trees. The grounds were impeccably kept with winding paths
bordered by whitewashed stones, flowers growing in profusion

overshadowed by several gigantic oaks. The house was of pink stucco in the Spanish style with low tiled roofs and a cool flagged patio in the center which seemed to be a garden in itself with innumerable potted plants flourishing around its borders.

Don Ramon met him at the threshold and extended his hand. "Welcome to our modest home, Señor."

"How do you do, sir. This really smacks of imposition, as I told your daughter yesterday."

"On the contrary. You saved my life. I made the mistake of rearing my daughters in the American tradition and I find that they lie in wait and tyrannize me on every pretext. They should be beaten with rattan every night for the good of their souls."

Don Ramon was a thin aristocratic man who stood over six feet tall, faultlessly dressed and every inch a Don. The austerity of his appearance was mitigated by the humor that lurked in the corners of his eyes and the full sensual lips that laughed easily.

"Pepé, take Señor Gerdt's baggage to the guest room and tell Lolita that we will have coffee in the patio. I trust coffee does not come too soon after breakfast. I assume that you have eaten."

"I have, but I never turn it down after fifteen months of service coffee. I breakfasted with Captain Soldarez."

Don Ramon's fine lips split in a smile. "Ah, yes. You would have met my illustrious nephew. A remarkable man, an unusual man."

He led the way to the patio and held a comfortable cushioned chair for Don, took one himself and lit a long black cigarette.

"I could see that. Why does he stay in a small town with his obvious talents?"

"Possibly for the same reason I do, although I slaved on the marts for years before becoming intelligent enough to stop and retire to live in peace. I revere the United States greatly, but the pace is too great. Here it is more leisurely. Ah, a daughter performs a touching bit of filial respect—pinch-hitting for Lolita, doubtless, because of the three she alone had not met you."

"Esta, may I present Señor Donald Gerdt of Texas."

Esta's dark penetrating eyes rested upon his for a moment, then she placed the coffee table between them and poured the dark fragrant brew from a silver pitcher. She did not speak.

Don, who had frozen at the remarkable statement by Don Ramon that Esta alone of three daughters hadn't met him, did not speak either.

"She talks little," said the older man as he offered Don cream and sugar. "The others more than make up for it." She stood in front of Don for a moment, a fabulously curved figure, dark skinned, her unfathomable eyes smouldering and her petulant lips full and damp and luscious, then she turned with a grace that made him think of an acrobat and disappeared.

"You say I met another one?" asked Don in a choked voice that he had to direct by main strength.

"Yes. Thereze told me that Felipe introduced you last evening at the hotel. Deldee was infuriated and might have pulled her hair, but it was at the breakfast table and I do manage to preserve some order at my own board."

Don relaxed, sweating, though the patio was cool. "Yes. I was wondering—I met so many people. I remember now. She wore a scarlet blouse and a figured skirt."

"I really don't know. I rarely see them except when they want something. The American rearing, you know. Is your stay limited, Mr. Gerdt?"

"You can call me Don, sir. My stay was indefinite to begin with and Phil has made it more so. In fact, I hardly know what to do with my time."

"I think Pepé has plans for that. He prevailed on me to fill his tank with gasoline last evening."

"Well, from now on I'll fill it for him. While we're on the subject I'm prepared to pay your price for putting me up."

Don Ramon shrugged. "We will speak of that when the time comes. I shall be most reasonable."

"Don't be too reasonable. I'm working for a rich woman and it won't be coming out of my pocket."

"You say Felipe has placed a fog on the length of your stay?"

"Yes." He shrugged. There was no reason why the old man shouldn't know what he was here for. "Mrs. Caraway doesn't believe it was her husband who was killed in the plane crash."

"Ah, so? And you are here to try to ascertain the facts?"

"That's about it. But Phil says to lay off the search until he gives the word."

The other puffed in silence for a while. "Without any further questions I urge you to do as he asks. I have known him since a child and I never heard him make a foolish request."

"I've already promised. He must be on something big."

"As to that, I could not say. I do say that if he made the request you would do well to abide by it."

"I shall, of course. If you don't mind, sir, I'd like to go to my room and put my things in order. Some of my clothes are pretty wrinkled."

"Have Deldee bring them to her mother. My Maris is a wizard with clothes, especially since I bought her an electric presser."

"Now, look," said Don positively. "I'm not going to make my stay here a drudge for Mrs. Cortez. There must be some place in town that will do my clothes."

"There is, of course, but I warn you not to deprive Maris of an opportunity to use her electric presser or her washing machine. She'd be cut to the quick."

Pepé, hovering nearby with a magazine in his hands beckoned and Don followed him to the room he was to occupy.

Deldee was there, clad in skin-tight white shorts and a short tailed purple shirt that missed the top of her shorts by several inches. The sleeves fitted her wrists tightly and bagged voluminously.

A raking thrust of appreciation skated through his nerves as she turned, her breasts punching sharply against the soft cloth of her shirt. His valises were open and she had put most of his stuff away.

Her face lighted and her smile was such that his throat seemed to grow stiff and full. "I took the liberty, Señor Don, of putting your clothes away. But I don't seem to find any—underclothes."

Her face turned faintly pink as he laughed. "You didn't find any because I don't wear them. No pajamas, either."

She caught her breath and bit her under lip as her face grew redder.

"She doesn't wear much of anything either, Señor Don," said Pepé quietly. "As you can see there is nothing under the shirt and she rarely sleeps in anything but her skin."

"Pepé!" Her embarrassment was acute. "You leave the room this minute."

"Not until Señor Don—if he would be so kind—autographs his picture."

Don's eyebrows went up. "Picture? What picture?"

"Here, sir. In *Life*"

He looked and saw Buzz Sawyer, Bucky Walters, Tinny Tinker and the rest of his gang standing in a group ready to take off the carrier, dressed in bulky flying garb with parachutes and Mae Wests in their hands. Don was uncomfortable, but took his pen and autographed the picture. Pepé read the inscription aloud.

"To my good friend Pepé with whom I expect to have some good times." He looked adoringly at Don and ran out of the room.

Don turned to Deldee who had recovered somewhat, but her face was still pink. "So you managed it?"

Her smile turned itself on like a light. "I told you."

He turned, slowly closed the door and came back, walking close to her, holding her eyes with his. "Now," he asked quietly. "Why?"

Her breath fluttered. "I thought I told you. I like you. I want to know you better."

He sighed and sat on a chair that was done in rustic cedar wood and bound with rawhide thongs. "I feel a responsibility, Deldee, that's sort of a nagging thing. I had just about made up my mind not to take your father up on his offer. You see, thrown with you like this every day—"

"You're afraid you'll fall in love with me," she said breathlessly.

"That, of course, is possible, but suppose you fell in love with me?"

She put her hands to her face and squeezed it slowly. "I'm afraid, Señor Don—I'm afraid I already have."

"No. You don't know me well enough. What you feel is a physical thing."

"Is that bad?"

"Depending on what your moral scruples are. I might fall in love with you, but suppose I didn't?"

She took her hands down, fell to her knees and sat on her feet. Her hands rested limply on her downy smooth thighs. "I don't know. I don't know," she whispered, her eyes flooding with tears. "There are so many things I don't know. I've been forward and maybe sinful in trying to get you here." Her head drooped and her hair fell forward, pouring over her shoulders in masses of raven glory.

Don was acutely embarrassed. He didn't know what to tell her, what to say to ease the turmoil in her breast. He reached out, caught her hands and placed them on his knees and held them tightly.

"Deldee, I wouldn't hurt you for the world. But don't you see I might, being around here, underfoot all the time?"

"I know, but if we don't see each other how'll we ever know?"

"That's a pretty problem, all right."

"I know I'm terrible to put you in this position. You never told me you loved me or even could. You only told me you thought I was beautiful."

"And I meant it. I'm going to tell you something. I've been pretty badly hurt, Deldee, three times. Maybe I'm more afraid for myself than I am for you."

Her head came up, her long lashes wet with tears, her eyes holding an entreaty that made them hard to meet. "Is there more for you to be afraid of than there is for me?"

"I suppose not. You've never been hurt. I have. That might make a difference."

"Then you're not—I mean you don't want to know—?" She drew herself up and leaned on his knees. "Señor Don, do you think I would hurt you?"

As though a switch had been thrown, he forgot about such things as consequences, troubles, turmoil and other matters that could not hold ground with her faintly perfumed nearness, the inky richness of her hair, the troubled entreating depths of her eyes, the tremulous twist to her lips and the warm pressure of her thinly clad breasts against his knees.

"Señor Don, you—" And she was in his arms, her head cradled in the crook of his elbow, her warm palpitant body trembling in his lap. For one aching moment he looked into her startled but passion-glazed eyes, then touched her lips with his. She responded with a hard muscular shudder, then her arms went around his neck and her mouth that had been stiff with tension and surprise went soft and lax. For a moment he gently tasted the lubricous smoothness of hers, drinking in the tiny muscular twitches that endowed her lips with lives of their own. His arms grew harder and a little moan came from deep in her throat as the questing tip of his tongue met hers. She started, her body growing hard from the shock, then with a lithe twist and leap she sprang from his arms and was gone.

He bent his head forward and rested it on the doubled fists on his knees and fought valiantly to quell the lashing fire the girl had injected into his veins.

A voice in soft Spanish impinged upon his consciousness, but he couldn't collect his thoughts sufficiently for a moment for it to make any impression.

Finally he raised his head and saw the woman standing before him clad in the voluminous clothes of a Mexican housewife.

She spoke again. "She will recover, Señor. I think she was overcome."

He stared at her stupidly for a moment, his tongue numb in his mouth. "I regret that I do not speak English," she said sadly and turned to go.

"No," he said in a strained voice. "Don't go. I speak Spanish after a fashion. I am bitterly sorry that you saw the kiss, Señora Cortez. In your own house, your own daughter—"

"It is the gentleman in you that speaks," she said, smiling softly. "You need not try to protect my daughter. Such things would not have been tolerated in my day, but this is another time. They were born in the United States and enjoy the privileges of American women. I think I know something of what you must feel, but do not feel badly. You cannot take all the responsibility upon yourself. She has told me all."

He blinked and swallowed noisily. "You are more than kind. I can hardly believe I'm in Mexico."

"What happened," she said with her ready smile, "could hardly have been avoided. I'm afraid my daughters are hot-blooded."

"Señora, do you not dear the effect of my presence in your house?"

"No, I do not. Think for a moment what would happen if you were less a gentleman."

"But you don't know anything about that. You can't. I might be the very person you think I am not."

She shook her head. "You don't understand what I mean, Señor Don. I do not expect gentlemanliness to overweigh the humanity in you. I know my daughters are attractive. One might even be called loose, but she is also intelligent. She knows exactly what she wants and she knows the penalities to be expected. You could not change her. You could not change Esta and you couldn't change Deldee. At the same time, neither could they change you. You are a gentleman and this I do know. You would not intentionally harm my daughters, nor would you expose them to physical dangers. You will do the best you can with them. What man could do more and still be a man?"

He shook his head in bafflement. "You are an extraordinary woman, Doña Maris."

She chuckled. "I, too, have been to the United States for many years. I have an extraordinary husband and four extraordinary children."

CHAPTER SEVEN

SHE LEFT him then, a prey to a landslide of cubist designs that marched through his mind without order and without reason. The voice of Pepé aroused him.

"Señor Don, shall we ride and view the countryside this morning?"

He stood up and looked the boy over more closely than he had before. He was a slim, delicately constructed lad with a sensitive face and limbs that, though frail-looking, held a suggestion of lithe whipcord strength. Like his sisters, his skin was smooth, almost effeminate.

"Sure, Pepé. Where shall we go?"

Pepé winked and came closer. "I know the valley like my hand. Shall I show you about?"

"That'd be best. I don't know anything about this part of the country. Do you have plenty of gas?"

"Yes, sir. Maybe I need a little oil. That last ring job I did didn't hold up too well."

The roads around thé valley were in decent condition, and they made good time. He was struck with the productivity of the small farms, the general air of prosperity, and the happy, well-fed appearance of the people. They came to the river and followed it up into the mountains where it rushed through rocky gorges and wound ever upward in a series of low falls toward the snowcaps where it had its birth. Finally about three thousand feet above the valley floor Pepé turned off on a side road and stopped.

"Why are you stopping?" asked Don.

"My cousin has forbidden that I go further."

"You mean Phil?"

"Yes, sir."

"What's up further?"

"I am not to tell you, sir."

"Oh? Where are the mines located? I'd like to see them."

Pepé was in a quandary. He was faced with a problem that might have caused more mature minds to pause. Finally, seeing that he did not have to break the letter of the order he blurted, "The mines are up ahead."

"Ah, I see."

"You won't tell Captain Soldarez I told you? I had to tell you something."

"No, I won't say anything to him. It's all very mysterious."

Pepé, feeling that he was safe, agreed with a nod. "He doesn't tell it, but I think he is waiting for something big to happen and I do know that he has stopped the people from picking around the silver mine. It is worn out, but the makers of trinkets find enough good ore to make their living."

"And he stopped them from going up there?"

"Yes, sir. You won't tell?"

"Indeed not. You may be a big help to me."

"Would you like a swim?"

"I'd love it. I see it can get hot in the valley."

No matter how hot it got in the valley, the clear foaming pool at the base of the falls where Pepé led him to swim was without a doubt the coldest water Don had ever dunked himself into in his life. It rammed through his vitals, making him gasp and flounder like an anxious fish. He swam across, whirled and came back at a racing crawl and, feeling sand under his feet, fled the water as though snakes were after him.

"Ohhh, brother, is that water cold."

"The best for swimming, Señor Don," said Pepé, his teeth chattering. "Warm water makes for tired."

"How did you happen to pick this particular pool, Pepé? Looks like it'd be better swimming further down where the water is warmer."

"There are good places further down and as you say they are warmer, but across the river but half a mile is my father's camp and the Tazapa family."

"I take it," said Don as he shivered into his clothes, "that the Tazapa family includes girls."

Pepé revealed his white teeth in a smile. "Such girls as you should be glad to meet."

"Why?" asked Don guardedly.

"Shall we go over and see?"

Feeling that he should put a halt to exploration, Don nevertheless nodded. Though he felt a slight chill of apprehension he allowed the now bubbling Pepé to lead the way to the car.

They went down the mountain road for several hundred yards, then turned off and approached the river where it flowed gently across hard graveled bars hardly six inches deep. The Ford had no trouble navigating the shallow water under the expert hand of Pepé, and soon they had climbed the opposite bank. After a hard steep climb they dipped over into a little wooded valley that seemed a green paradise in the midst of a wilderness of rock.

Don stifled an exclamation of pleased surprise at the sight. The valley was hardly a mile long and about half that wide with sheer cliffs rising like forts on either side. At the far end a tiny waterfall sent a ribbon of water through a crevice in the rock wall and to their left he could see the small stream scuttling on its way to the larger river.

"There is the camp," said Pepe, pointing.

A hundred yards ahead was a broad-fronted old house constructed of natural rock and cedar logs with a front porch the full width of the house. The windows were glazed and there was a chimney of rock at each end. The sight of it was restful to the eyes and the tension set in action by Pepé's words about the girls, seemed to slip away from Don. What could happen in a place like this?

"Where are the girls?" he asked, instantly wishing he had remained silent.

"They'll be here as soon as they hear the car." He goosed the motor into a shattering roar and turned the ignition key. "They live around a turn in the road. Their parents keep the place for us and raise corn and vegetables for their own table. They have a few cows too."

"Aren't you afraid of the parents?"

"Oh, no. The old man is blind and the old woman has arthritis in her legs and can't walk far."

Don laughed. "Then you really have a love nest here."

Pepé rolled his eyes amorously. "Maybe it could be improved, but I don't know how. Three women are better than one any day."

"Holy mackerel! Not three at once?"

"Oh yes, sir. It is quite a novelty."

"I can imagine," commented Don, getting out of the car and feeling a little chill.

Pepé opened the house which was not locked and walked in, Don behind him. The central room was large and roughly but comfortably furnished with deer hides on the floor, comfortable chairs with rawhide bottoms, antlers on the walls and a huge bed-like divan that was covered with cushions and a big rug of native Indian make.

There came a patter of bare feet and feminine giggles down the trail, and into the house burst three girls so exactly alike that they couldn't have been anything but triplets, and so tenderly fleshed that they couldn't have been very old. They slid to a stop in the doorway when they saw Don and for a moment stood there in embarrassed silence. They were small but deliciously curved, their faces revealing a strong Indian mixture, their cheek bones high and their eyes slightly oblique. Their hair was coal black, bobbed in a point on the forehead and shingled behind, a manner

Don thought peculiar. They were dressed in scarlet cotton skirts with blouses that cut across the arms below the shoulders and fell quite low in front.

"Hi," said Pepé grandly. "You needn't be afraid of Señor Don. He is my friend. He fought in Korea and got the Congressional Medal of Honor. He's a pilot."

They tittered and came into the room, casting shy glances at him; then they all began spouting Spanish at Pepé, asking him questions that made Don's face flame.

Pepé grinned and said, "He speaks Spanish, you idiots."

They screamed at the news and the foremost questioner ran and flung herself across the couch in an agony of embarrassment and mirth, her skirt flying up and giving Don a peek at sturdy round limbs clad in skin of mouth-watering softness.

"Is ... " He cleared his throat. "Is there a drink in the house, Pepé?"

"Yes, sir. Tequila. My father drinks nothing else."

"Bring it out. Right now I could use some."

He used some, then some more so that by the time the girls lost their awe of him, he was feeling mellow and friendly.

"You probably won't be able to tell them apart," said Pepé, "but—" He pointed them out. "This is Ynez and this is Yma and this is Yolanda. They came from San Antonio when their father's eyes were put out in a gas explosion."

Ynez, the one who had revealed herself by diving to the couch, came and sat on the floor near Don's feet. Her eyes were almost jet black and her face was elfin, with red lips that always seemed ready to laugh. Pepé was wrestling playfully with the other two on the couch —although to Don his play seemed to have an object.

Ynez smiled up at Don. "Do you like me, Señor?"

He laughed. "Of course. What man wouldn't like a girl so beautiful? Even if she does like to ask embarrassing questions about strangers."

She gasped and giggled, turning her face that had become a dusky red. "I did not know you spoke Spanish. I'm sorry."

"Don't be. I was amused."

A gasp followed by a giggle from the couch made him look up and gulp audibly. Pepé had nearly stripped one of the girls and the other one was helping him, smothering her laughter. The one being disrobed was essaying a very intimate bit of teasing on Pepé and didn't seem to mind the operation in the least.

Don gulped again and stood up. "I think Pepé needs privacy. I think I'll step into the next room."

Ynez stood up hydraulically, it seemed, caught his arm and squeezed herself close. "I'll go with you."

He assented since there seemed no alternative; besides, either the girl or the tequila was speeding curious sensations about his body. Inside the door she swung around in front of him, her face upturned and her breath coming fast. "I hear Americans kiss beautifully, Señor."

He bent and kissed her without pausing to think it over and found that whatever the Americans could do with the kiss she was not in the least ignorant of it. Don staggered toward the nearest support which proved to be the bed. He collapsed upon it, bringing her with him, a wild ravenous ball of T.N.T.

From then on Don's recollection of that day was patchwork and clouded by fantasy that he knew was not fantasy but his own inability to imagine any such thing. She was a wildcat whose demand was savage, whose heights lasted a very short while; after collapsing and gasping out her fatigue her lips would begin to roam and with it would come another surge of passion which he always seemed to match. He remembered a short interval during which she brought him a staggering drink of tequila and cold water. Later it seemed that there were two of them, then three people that were one.

The Ford hummed downgrade toward the valley being tooled around curves and over rises by the sure hand of Pepé.

"Was not the day enjoyed, Señor Don?"

Don groaned and forced himself erect in the seat. "Pepé, you are the most incarnate devil ever whelped. I doubt that anyone but you could have ever dreamed up something like I just barely survived."

Pepé giggled. "Did I not say that three were better than one?"

"You didn't mention anything about the morality rate of such endeavors."

Pepé did not quite understand and laughed aloud. "The triplets are women among women."

"Amen, brother—although we might not be speaking of the same thing."

"I think we are."

Don thought it possible but skidded down in the seat and promptly went to sleep.

Dinner that night was a meal mixed with such emotional fever that when it was over Don hardly remembered what he had eaten.

Esta stared at him so continuously that he wanted to flee. Deldee did not look at him at all and Thereze, when she did look, was smug and emanated the unspoken words, "Another time is just around the corner."

Don Ramon conversed effortlessly in faultless English and Dona Maris put in occasionally with Spanish.

Don, with some several million half-formed thoughts marching in a steady parade through his mind, found it possible to uphold some semblance of conversation. Pepé thankfully kept his silence, ate voraciously and shot only a few fraternal glances at his hero.

It was twilight in a cloudless sky when Captain Soldarez drove by in a Sunbeam Talbot sports car and picked Don up for a spin in the cool of the evening.

"Did Pepé take you on one of his amorous safaris?"

Don started. "You mean it's common knowledge?"

"My good fellow, I am the repository of more out of the .way knowledge than you have any idea. Just because I know it doesn't make it common knowledge."

"I'm sorry. I forgot for the moment that you are the police and probably know everything that goes on hereabouts."

Phil laughed exuberantly. "I have a spy system that's a dilly. You should see it in operation. For instance, I know that you kissed Deldee this a.m. and it so shattered her that even yet she is not recovered."

Don blushed becomingly. "You're a devil, Phil."

"By no means. No man finds anything out by himself. I think you're sharp enough to know that the bare fact of her fleeing so precipitously speaks volumes for yourself in the clinch."

"Oh, nuts. Say, where did that trio of Jezebels come from at Don Ramon's camp?"

"Destitute cousins. Distantly. They were in San Antonio and, the father was blinded by a natural gas explosion. The mother had a beauty shop but when the old man lost his sight her creditors grew jittery and closed in on her. Don Ramon and myself bailed her out and brought them down here."

"Then that's where they got those haircuts?"

"I suppose so. She was supposed to be quite good in a small way. The old people are happy and secure but I rather feel sorry for the children. That's no place for three hot-blooded youngsters."

"Hot-blooded? That's an understatement, brother. They're boiling lava."

"By the way, Dariel is coming down."

"Oh, no!"

"Oh, yes. You should be overjoyed."

"Why?"

"You once told me you were considering marrying her."

"You penetrated that bit of falsehood without any trouble."

"Another spot of information came in today, too. Your dossier from Washington. Hero, Airman, All Southwestern end at Texas A and M. Majored in engineering. German parentage mixed with French and Italian. Background as American as Zapata is Mexican. Spotless. Congratulations."

"Thanks and what's this leading up to?"

Phil swung the Sunbeam away from town and toward the mountains. "Don, it's about time you were broken in on some dope I've got tucked away. You left Korea and came here to sit right on the lip of a powder keg."

"Go on."

Phil ran a slim finger beneath his moustache and frowned. "It's hard to tell you because there are many details that I lack. Actually, I know that a monster steal is mounting right here under my nose and until there is some break I can't do a thing."

"What sort of a steal?"

"A steal of such proportion that if it is successful might alter the course of history."

"You almost convince me. What is it, a mine producing pure refined plutonium?"

"You may scoff. Don, what do you know of the process of nuclear fission? The production of radioactive isotopes, plutonium—stuff like that."

"I know about as much as the triplets up at the camp, so be as esoteric as you please."

"I shall strive not to be. Actually, I know little more than you, except that I became interested when several men bounced in here one day and offered hard cash for the workings of a stripped silver mine. Not enough cash to look suspicious but enough to assure a prompt acceptance. It is a government-owned mine and I received an order to keep the native silversmiths from the area. Being by nature a suspicious soul, I took off up there before they got their workers in and made off with a rock of every sort I could find, then went to Mexico City with my boodle. I know a geologist lad there who knows a physicist and we put our heads together coming up with a headache, king size. Did you ever hear of a chemical called corium-2?"

"No. Is there one?"

Phil massaged his face and nodded. "I'm not too clear just what the chemical status of the stuff is, but I do know that when used it replaces several costly and tedious steps in the production of plutonium. In fact, this physicist said that it could mean in Russian hands the end of Western supremacy in the production of atomic materials. There are only two known deposits at the present time. One in the Belgian Congo and one in Canada. That places it all on our side. Even so, there is not enough for use as they'd like to use it. The samples I took to the geologist were hot with it and on assay it is about ten times as rich as any other deposit —percentage wise, I mean. It doesn't exist in the pure state."

"Well, with Mexico having this deposit, then we have it all."

Phil chuckled thoughtfully. "Should be that way, shouldn't it? The trouble is, they—I mean those who stand to get a good cut of backsheesh out of this—would take good care that those higher up didn't learn why a silver mine where there is no silver of significance was sold at a fat figure. It happens all the time. Say, I'd go to some middle strata government official and announce that I'd learned how to get a lot of silver out of very low grade ore. Not much, mind you, but enough to make it profitable. Let me have this old dud of a mine and I'll make money for both of us but keep the peons away because they not only take out ore, but they might let someone in on my process and there'd go my profit and your profit plus sending others in a mad rush with my process to work over every old diggings in the country. So I get an official pat on the back by the right palms, pitch in and dig out a million, two million—or ten—and be off with it if it became necessary to be off. All this time the upper echelons of government are ignorant of what goes. Except occasionally there is a Soldarez."

"Well, in any event we'd get it in the end, wouldn't we?"

The other's face grew wooden. "What assurance do we have that Russia won't get it?"

Don sat up and peered at Soldarez through slitted eyes. "You must know something more."

"I do. Lots. Naturally, nothing that goes on up there is missed by my spies who watch from the mountainsides with binos taking care that the sun doesn't strike them. Nevertheless, I've lost two men. Vanished without a trace."

"And, of course, they were sweated unmercifully and told everything they knew."

Phil's grin was Mephistophelean. "They told nothing because they knew nothing. Their orders are to observe and report. Nothing more."

"And what has been reported?"

"Well, to drop back a ways we must include the luscious Carol. It is obvious that she was sent here to find out things. She didn't, of course, but not for want of trying. Would you say she is a denizen of our part of the world?"

"No. I had her tabbed as Continental."

"As did I. I'll even go so far as to tag her as some Balkan gal. Women of her caliber simply do not haunt the apartments of obscure police officials to display their wares on first assault. Think for a moment, Don—a sophisticated beautiful woman must have to be thoroughly indoctrinated to some high cause to thus give herself to a man with no other reason than to dig him for information."

"I see what you're driving at all right, but you're ignoring two things. You're the sort of a bird who might make the church warden's daughter part with her virtue and gladly. Second, this gal might just like to play in bed."

The grin was borrowed from Beelzebub. "You flatter my poor talents,"

"I'll bet! Nevertheless, I'm inclined to go along with your assessment. Since her interests are at first glance foreign and she doesn't back away from anything to gain her point, then I take it that you have her tabbed as a Russian or one of the Iron Curtain country helpmates?"

"Something like that, although I'm necessarily a little elastic yet because I just don't know. I have more than a suspicion that Caraway is involved because his mining properties abutt those the government leased and his disappearances came a fortnight after we had the visit from their agents. It is entirely likely that the material extends in strata into Caraway's property. I was thinking about that when I discovered that the burned corpse wasn't the McCoy. With my imaginings I could conceive of a coup so big and with such far-reaching repercussions as to stagger the mind."

"What do your superiors think of the matter?"

"I've had my wrist slapped once. Happily, I don't have to worry about it."

"How's that?"

"Maybe you've seen one of these and maybe you haven't. They're issued by your government to a very select few men all over the world and I don't think a better idea ever flourished. With this in my pocket I go straight to the president if I have to."

He took out a pigskin wallet, delved into a secret compartment and handed Don a stiff card.

He took one look and felt a strange thrill ripple through his nerves. He had seen one, and the automaton who had carried it he had known since World War II as one of the coldest, most objective killers of his experience. High in the brass of the OSS he had spurred revolutions behind enemy lines in half a dozen countries. A man of silent mien, a machine whose chilly eyes were all that suggested his implacability.

He handed it back almost with humility. "Yes, I saw one once. Used to be a fellow Marine, some time ago."

"You mean Norcross?"

"Yes. Do you know him?"

"I should. I dropped him in Yugoslavia in 'forty-two. That man is an icicle and I didn't even think he liked me, but we had several brushes and nearly got it a couple of times. In fact, I landed him under fire and had to take off right into it. Lucky! He recommended me for this honor. I think there are about thirty of us, maybe fifty in the world. The idea stemmed from that man among men in Washington of your F.B.I. Roosevelt, who was one to smell a good idea a long way off, implemented it for him. The idea is that a nucleus of us, well-scattered in your country and mine as well as all over the world could in time of extreme peril gather a force of men. The original idea was a sort of self-energizing thing where every man I picked would also pick men he could trust beyond any possible doubt, amounting to roughly ten thousand men whose objective would be to work in coopera-tion with the forces of other men like me. Armed, trained and absolutely trustworthy, dedicated to the retention of freedom and democratic ideals. A formidable force could be lined up that way and the manner in which these few were picked is the best insurance against duds. When I was interviewed they were even aware that I had once thrashed the b'jesus out of the leader of the gang who eliminated Trotzky—although at the time had I known I had tackled a scorpion I'd have let him go in a hurry, I tell you. They had me tabbed from the cradle up. For my part, working through men like Don Ramon and a hundred others I know whose integrity is beyond question, I could gather a force in three days that'd make someone's eyes pop."

"How would you arm them?"

"That poses a problem but there is a system worked out by which your own country would do it. It has flaws, but I think it'd work. The arms are at the moment in secret caches known to very few people and they would be flown at an instant's notice anywhere. Now that we—I identify my own fate with that of the United States unconsciously, you see—have bases all over, the problem is simplified.'"

"Then you're a bigger wheel than I thought."

He shrugged and snapped on the fights. "That little card, Don," he said soberly, "makes me feel bigger than any medal I got in the war. I'll tell you—"

The Sunbeam whipped and skidded in answer to locked brakes missing the rocky shoulder of the road by inches but scraping the back fender of the Buick that had charged them wide open and head on. The Buick skidded wildly and crashed side on into a boulder just a few feet off the road.

"That," said Phil, leaving the car in a fluid bound, "was intentional." There was a flash of silver and two thundering reports rent the still night air. One shot came from the car and was answered by two more shots from Phil's big nickled Colt. "In the glove compartment, Don. Gun and flashlight."

Don banged open the compartment and came out with a long-barreled Luger and a flashlight.

"Flash it on the car."

In the illumination they could see the form of the driver sprawled on his face through the open door, his feet still in the car. A man who had been sitting beside the driver was making fumbling motions at his chest, blood pouring in roping blobs from his gasping mouth.

"Care," snapped Phil crisply. "There's a third."

They approached the car slowly, side by side. Ten feet away a man sprang erect on the back seat and a German Schmeisser belched one slug. The Colt flashed up, spent its last two cartridges in the man's chest and the Schmeisser burped away, tearing out hunks of upholstery, sawing through the man on the front seat, knocking him forward into the dash where he hung for a moment, then fell sideways to the floor.

CHAPTER EIGHT

PHIL SLIPPED cartridges into his revolver in a steady click-ing stream and with a whip of his wrist snapped the cylinder home. "All, I believe," he said easily. "Question. Who were they after?"

"You! They have no reason to be after me. You can scotch the works and you're better off dead."

"They caught us in a curve and were going too fast. That's why they skidded. My Sunbeam is quicker to answer the wheel."

"I wouldn't have given a two penny stamp in either case. I could see us crashing the wall and car too."

"I handle a car fairly well," said Phil, modestly. "I'll unlim-ber my short wave and have some of my men pick this up. Now the hair will fly from some direction. Tomorrow, you become a deputy—no, tonight. You have a gun?"

"Yeah, a .45 I stole. That's my baby."

"All right. You're not to go to the John without it. Don't go wandering around with Pepé unless you have someone else along. Someone like..." He frowned and concentrated. "I have just the man."

"Who?"

"One of my men. He's the breath of discretion and he won't interfere with you and Pepé. He's a rifle 105prodigy and won't carry sidearms. One of my top troubleshooters."

It was late when Don got back to the Cortez home. He joined the family in the patio where they had gathered to drink cooling fruit juices and talk. Esta alone was missing. He did not mention the brush he and Phil had had because he didn't care to discuss it, being unaccountably depressed.

"May I offer you tequila or whiskey, Señor Don?" asked Thereze.

"Yes, please. Whiskey with water and as much as you think one man could stand at one drink."

Don Ramon chuckled. "You sound like a man with something to forget, Señor Don."

"I suppose so. I'm a little low tonight. Phil and I have been riding and he explained a lot."

"Ah, so? We are quite proud of our nephew. I could offer you no better advice than to bow to his wishes since I take it there might be some danger to your person involved. I make bold to suggest that some damage, to the heart possibly, has already been done."

"Father, I don't think Señor Don would care to talk about his troubles," put in Deldee from her dark corner.

Don Ramon laughed softly. "He is a man and should he choose not to speak he has only to say so."

Don nodded. "That's right. True, I always seem to get myself in the way of emotional landslides, but I think it comes like luck at cards."

"Tactics," said Don Ramon, "that do not take the nature of the enemy's force into account will prove lacking."

"I'm sure Señor Don does not consider the women in his life in the nature of an enemy," said Deldee somewhat acidly.

"That depends," said Don. "In the past they have appeared that way. Not as enemies, possibly, but certainly people who wished me no good to the point that they'd do me considerable harm."

After the drink was consumed, Don pleaded fatigue and retired, taking good care that his door was locked. He undressed then and went to bed, in the nude, as usual.

Half an hour later, having turned and tossed fretfully, feeling his liquor, he got up, turned on the bedlight and discovered a bottle of bourbon and a pitcher of water on the night table near his bed. He poured a huge drink and sat on the bed while he sipped it, relishing the warm bite of the liquor in his stomach.

The lock rattled faintly and he grinned at the door, mentally shaking hands with himself. He had already surpassed himself for one day and had no intention of setting a world's record.

As the fumes of the liquor mounted, he went to the window that opened out on the garden and raised the blinds so that any errant breeze would find its way in, then went back to the bed and continued to drink.

Another half hour passed and Don felt as though he might be able to sleep; he was slightly drunk. He was reaching for the light switch when he heard a rustle in the big mimosa outside his window. He froze for a moment and cursed not having—put the automatic under his pillow. Without warning a slim body shot through the window and landed with a soft thud on the tile floor of his bedroom. It was Esta, her breasts heaving with increased breathing, her dark eyes hot and smouldering. She was dressed in dark purple shorts that fit like skin, and a blousy shirt of thin material that ballooned about the sleeves and torso but could not obscure the outlines of her breasts.

"Good evening, Señor Don," she said shyly, her lips widening in a slow provocative smile.

"Esta, you shouldn't be here. The family might ... He yanked the corner of a sheet over his middle.

"They've gone to bed. I always stay out late."

"But why—?"

"You think my sisters are beautiful and have told them so. Do you not think I also am beautiful?"

"I do." Again he felt the situation slipping from his grasp and the skin on his back reacting in a manner that made him want to squirm.

She walked slowly over and sat beside him on the bed, sending to his nostrils a bewitching perfume that made his heart pump furiously.

"May I taste your drink?"

He handed it to her, dumbly feeling the electric emanations that seemed to spring from her pores like a fragrance rated in volts. It was two-thirds of a hefty drink that he had about decided to let go dead, but the girl downed it in one gulp, went to the bottle, poured herself half a glassful and added a little water. Like water she drank it, wandering silently about the room, her hips rolling with gracefully controlled seductiveness, her legs shimmering like oiled velvet in the dim illumination. Don sat and watched her, his skin prickling with detached wonder, his brain held in the rhythm of her stride, his mind feeling locked in the deeply banked fires of her eyes that never left his. Like a man coming under the influence of a hypnotist he followed her stride until at last she had finished the third drink. She stopped and, placing her hands on her hips, stretched backward until her ribs stuck out and her breasts were stretched tightly against the shirt. One hand touched the floor, then the other, and her right leg, stiffly extended, rose slowly until it passed the zenith; then the other followed. She straightened up and hurled her heavy hair over her shoulders and smiled. "You like that, Señor Don?"

He nodded, not trusting himself to speak.

"Would you like to see me really dance for you?"

Again came the nod and without a word she turned and went through the window like a diver going into a deep pool. He winced, but heard only a light thud striking the ground below the window.

In minutes she was back via the same route by which she had entered. Still Don sat on the bed, chained by the terrific magnetism of the girl, the maddening grace of her movements and the witchery of her eyes. Fleetingly the thought raced through his mind that since getting on the bus after the plane ride he had been not much more than a puppet put through its paces by a succession of extraordinary women who successfully twisted whatever he possessed in the way of Victorian perspective out of his grasp and bent him to their wills —not that the bending had been anything but delight of a very special sort.

She was now clad in a cape of some fragile stuff that was opaque enough to hide the most intimate details of her body but not enough to fog its luscious outlines, the oiled ease with which her limbs moved and the sweat-starting poetry of her hips that seemed to be booming drums telegraphing some ancient message in a strange but yet understandable language.

She came to him and touched his shoulders with her soft fingertips, drawing them down his arms and thighs, leaving a trail of sensation that made him exert will to keep from crying out.

Then she poured him a drink, handed it to him and touched her glass to his with a faint tinkle. "Drink to us, Señor Don, and the music we will make."

"Esta, I-"

"Drink!" It was not a request but an order and he hastened to obey.

She put the glasses down and did a quick lashing whirl that raised the cape and gave him a body that seemed glowing with an inner fire so utterly free and abandoned, so marvelously constructed and so wantonly exerted, that he shuddered from the drive of several sharply tuned emotions that seemed to sweep him in unison.

The cape dropped and smudged out detail again as she crept about in a half crouch, her face wildly savage. In the distance it seemed he could hear the muffled booming of native drums and then by some magic the room gradually changed until it was a half circle of jungle embracing a white beach. Don shook himself back to reality only to feel that he had done them both a disservice and let the the fantasy creep back, finding after a while that it was not only a lonely bit of white moon-drenched beach, but that he had been somehow drawn from his place and was following her, entering the spirit of the dance, being the chaser while she was the fleeing woman. Dampness began to spot her costume and finally with a despairing gesture she unsnapped the catch and hurled it from her, standing on tiptoe, her body glistening with sweat, palpitant and hurling at him a challenge that he was not long in taking. With a bound he seized her in his arms but she squirmed free and skidded away from him.

He caught her again and for a moment he held her, her body welding itself to him like a leech; then she whirled away again and skipped easily out of the way of his grasping hands. His muscles leaped and his chest heaved, his heart thudding powerfully in his chest. He was a savage man, unclad, about to take his woman who was teasingly just beyond reach. His spring put her in his grasp again. He found her lips and felt the bursting upsurge of her muscles as the power soared through her, making her a thing of writhing eagerness, but still determined to carry out the ritual. She was quiescent for a moment; then she began a snake-like movement that squirted her eel slick body out of his grasp. Trying to catch her, he fell to one knee. She fell across his back, slid down and over his knee with a serpentine twist, the wet trail of her skin swelling his throat with the desire to roar. Her arms went around his neck and she kissed him driving deep for the sweetness that was hard to reach, making his head roar and his nerves screech at the injustice. He got up and took her with him, still clinging like bark to a tree.

The night became a whirl of maddening sequences, of the frenzied wonders of her hot hungry lips, the eagerness of her flesh and the exorbitant power of her body.

The next morning Don woke with his head hot and feverish and his tongue a dry warped board in his mouth.

With a groan that advertised his misery he tottered to the bathroom where a needle shower that was spawned of the snow cap drove the cobwebs from his brain and excited his sluggish bloodstream into activity. Gasping but relieved, he stepped out and dried rapidly and abrasively on a big towel.

Still addlepated and mentally at loose ends he wandered out of the bathroom, scrubbing his head with a towel, and almost walked into Deldee who carried a tray of iced papaya juice. She gave a little muffled cry and Don, in an effort to cover up, struck himself in a highly sensitive spot and nearly fainted. He reeled to the bed, his towel draped unbecomingly but safely across his middle and almost gave in to the impulse to weep. This household had just about gotten the best of him. There had not been ten minutes in sequence when he was not beset by some disturbing element. He was beginning to wear thin.

"I brought you some juice," she said in a small voice. "I'm sorry about the way I acted."

He raised suffering eyes to hers and tried to smile. He wiped away the dismal effort, scowled savagely and was a great deal more successful. Then, feeling repentant and better, he sat up and accepted the juice from her. It was sweet and rich and as cold as ice, a boon to the fires in his stomach. When he had finished he felt up to civil conversation. "I'm sorry about that, too, Deldee, but I just couldn't help it. I just couldn't."

"Then maybe…"

He held up a hand that trembled. "Please—let's just let things rock along for a while, will you? I'll admit I couldn't resist you, but—" He couldn't tell her that he hadn't had any better luck with resistance in other fields either.

Suddenly she lost her temper and slammed tray and glass to the tile floor. "Don Gerdt, you're—you're a great big sniveling sissy!" She whirled, the act casting her skirt to a height that would have shocked her, and flew from the room.

He lifted a trembling hand and mopped his face. "And just when I thought things were about to level off."

At nine, after he had eaten breakfast, endured the combined stares of Thereze and Esta and wondered what Deldee was thinking, he was glad to hear the snort of Phil's Sunbeam as it ground up the graveled drive.

He hurried and got in before Phil had a chance to get out. "You," offered Phil, cheerily, "look like hell."

"Thanks," snapped Don bitterly. "You, I'm sorry to say, seem to be your usual buccaneering self."

"I am. Chipper as a sparrow. Unless I am mistaken we will adventure much today. Feel up to it?"

"I guess so. About the only thing I don't feel up to today is another meeting with Thereze, Esta, or the triplets."

"Ah. So you've made the rounds?"

"With about as little volition on my part as I ever accomplished anything worthwhile."

"Then you do not think them common or low simply because of their lusty natures and forward attitudes?"

"Oh, go soak your head. When you come down to it, in what way are they different from me? Change things a little and I could be put on the offensive, too. I never went much for the double standard. All it has to support it is ten thousand years of practice."

"And a spate of fundamental injustice that makes an intelligent mind retch. We're to meet the lovely Dariel this morning."

"Nope. Count me out."

"Can't, chum. You're a deputy now, remember? Moreover, this isn't going to be a usual meeting at all."

"How do you mean?"

"There is an airport in the mountains. One thought to be hidden and no planes have landed on it yet. It is a flat tableland with little brush on it and few boulders. It has been bulldozed clear and now a B-36 could land there and take off. From the space cleared they must expect a squadron of them. It is there I expect Dariel to land. If she doesn't then I'll be wrong. If she does I expect fun. Game?"

"In that case, yes. We're not bearding the lion alone, are we?"

"Ostensibly, yes. The field is not guarded because they don't know I know about it or else they have too few men." He glanced at a wrist chronometer. "In about thirty minutes there will be twenty riflemen stationed at strategic points around the up-wind end of the most likely looking strip. There are two machine guns as well, but they are there for a just-in-case measure. I don't expect to use them."

"A Hannibal, no less," breathed Don admiringly.

Phil shrugged. "Only a fool treads in a spot like this without first taking common precautions. I hope to live a full full life—and a long one."

"Then you think Dariel and her husband and the kingpins of this other group are hand in glove?"

"So I think. Just what their relationship is I don't know. There is one thing. If Caraway went to such lengths to prove himself dead—" He stroked his moustache while his face went hard. "He could be the moving spirit. Maybe he aspires to be a Fritz Mandel or a Krupp. I just don't know. I do know that we stand a good chance of missing if my superiors become bothersome. To obviate that I have invited *Señor Presidente* to pay us a visit."

"Will he do it? Did you let him know something big was afoot?"

"I did," Phil chuckled. "He's quite a guy, as you would say. He's no fool. He wired back in a matter of minutes. You see, it isn't generally known, but *el Presidente* was, during the last fracas, one Eddy Daviet. Maybe you've heard the name."

Don straightened up. "What is this? Did Mexico form some sort of foreign legion during the war, all under assumed names?"

"In a manner of speaking. We were twenty-six in number, all flyers. Merry England was glad to have us and we were glad to fly Spitfires instead of our old Curtiss P-35s."

The road led higher and higher and was now nothing but a trail. They had left the road Pepé and Don had traveled the day before, some miles back, and now the Sunbeam was turned into a mountain goat, navigating hairpin turns, avoiding dense patches of *cholla* and *seguaro,* boulders as big as a house, skirting canyons and being occasionally swallowed in dry coulees.

Gradually they were approaching the sawtoothed peaks beyond which lay the newly made air strips. "I'd like to see Dariel's face when we offer her a lift to town," said Don with bitter satisfaction.

"You will. Two to one she doesn't accept our invitation."

Don ground out a short harsh laugh. "For calculated shock this appearance of yours will be a super. She swoops in all ready to be armed up by her ever-loving and you skate up and offer her a lift just as though you were supposed to meet her."

"But I am. On the same bus by which you arrived."

"Then you seem mighty sure she'll come in by plane."

"A hunch. I think she intends to see Caraway, then just appear at the village with some story about missing the bus and being driven in by private conveyance."

"If you're right, I have a suggestion."

"By all means. What?"

"Let's don't appear. Let's hide and watch through binos. Let her see Caraway and get all briefed and come down to the village primed with whatever. Then she'll be at least primed to give even if she doesn't. If we bring her back she won't know anything and won't be able to do whatever she's coming to do. Whatever that is might be illuminating."

Phil laughed and smote the steering wheel. "My friend, I am supposed to be the clever one. Will you remember that in the future and let me make such suggestions? That is, of course, what we'll do. I must have been mad to think of anything else. Dariel is a clever, intelligent woman, but if she beats us we deserve beating."

He warmed up the short wave and barked *a* string of orders in Spanish into the microphone, listened, spoke briefly and cradled the instrument. "That will fix things. Ahl"

They had topped the last rise and below them was a vast rocky plateau that had been scraped as flat as a billiard table. Strips were laid out, outlined by boulders that had been rolled from the needed areas, along with brush and cactus. Phil had been right. On that pavement-like surface the heaviest plane in existence could land and take off.

"Now," he said. "What sort of planes do you suppose those strips were laid out for?"

"Not Cubs," said Don, searching the horizon and nearer spots for signs of habitation.

Phil rolled the Sunbeam into the shade of a gigantic boulder and stopped. They got out and unwound the neck straps of powerful glasses.

"To our back is a good spot. It's high and we can hide in the brush. I rather think they have binos, too."

"Had your men spotted anyone?"

"Not a soul. See that dark spot in the cliff wall to the north?"

"Yes."

"It's a tunnel. I think Caraway did that with just this idea in mind. It wasn't there two years ago. The wall where the tunnel is doesn't measure very thick and he had all the necessary equipment."

"What happened to his miners?"

"Discharged them and suspended operations a year ago. Mine petered out, he said. I tried to find his chief engineer, but couldn't. I'd like to know."

"So would I. About what time do you think she'll arrive?"

"That's hard to say. What time did you arrive in Villa Enriquez?"

"Right after noon."

"Then assuming she's traveling at the same speed she should get here between one-thirty and two. This distance by air is nothing. By bus it is something else."

Don looked at his watch, made a grimace and skidded back beneath a thick bush where the sun didn't penetrate. "Well, wake me when you see the whites of their eyes."

Tiny grey birds flitted about on noiseless wings in quest of insects, and twenty feet away a great iguana climbed to the crest of a boulder and seemed to stare at the sun. Soldarez threw a stone at him and he scuttled noisily away.

The sun climbed higher and Don snored louder while the other sat like a stone and smoked cigarettes. At onetwenty by the captain's watch, a faint drone came out of the north and in a short while he could see the silver wings of the plane glinting in the sunlight.

"Wake up, Don. Looks like I was right."

Don sat up, pawed the sleep from his eyes and squinted at the plane. "Looks like another Cessna 190."

"It is. Caraway must like them."

The plane swooped lower, passing them at eight hundred feet, and swung back into the wind and settled lightly to the strip, sending up a faint spurt of dust. It taxied up near the wall of the cliff and while they watched three vehicles emerged from the entrance of the tunnel.

There were two half tracks of World War II vintage and a jeep. The jeep scurried out on the strip and slid to a stop near the plane. The two half tracks pulled clear of the tunnel and stationed themselves on each side of the entrance.

"Take a look at those half tracks," said Phil.

Don trained his binoculars and stifled an exclamation. "Twenty millimeter guns!"

"Correction—40 millimeter guns. The only place I ever saw them short-barreled and in braces was on shipboard. I'd say they're pretty effective artillery and Caraway doesn't pass up any bets. Ah, the beauteous Dariel."

There was no mistaking the amazonian elegance of the woman that stepped from the plane clad in slacks and tight T-shirt. Even from a distance the provocative insurgence of her breasts was easily discernible. Don went tense and remained so until his shirt was bathed with sweat; he sank back then and let the binoculars dangle.

"Well, there she is," he said in a peculiar voice which made Phil glance anxiously at him.

"Yes. There she is. Thanks to you, we can now go back and wonder what her next move will be. I don't suppose there's any further reason to doubt that she and her husband are in league. That was the lanky man with the baseball cap who kissed her. He didn't look very dead, did he?"

"No, but I still don't get it. A man with his money—"

"Is the man who can envision more," said Phil. "Especially since he knows how to make it."

"Yeah. Dariel said he always told her he could take two hundred thousand and climb right back in the millionaire ranks."

"I'd bet on it. Shall we go?"

CHAPTER NINE

L ATE THAT afternoon Don sat- in his room after a bath and a change of clothes and took stock as sanely as he could. Dariel's arrival had upset him, but now even though he could look at the situation with the same cold eye as Soldarez, he doubted that he could do what the captain had asked. To greet her and act as though he had seen nothing through the window of the plane would take a spot of doing.

After supper he received a phone call of which Deldee informed him in distinctly chilly tones.

"Señor Don, there is a woman to speak with you." Having delivered her message she whirled and stalked off with him behind her.

"Don! Darling!" The old music was there and Don's heart took a great leap, then fell back to its normal rhythm.

"Yes? Say, isn't this Dariel?" His tones sounded so spurious he felt his face growing hot.

"Well, I must say you don't sound very pleased."

"I'm overcome. If you remember I wanted you to come along in the first place. What's the trouble?"

"Nothing. I just wanted to see you. Can you come up to the hotel about eight?"

"Sure. Earlier than that if you say the word." Boy, but I sound terrible, he thought.

"No. I have to get the travel off me. Those busses—you should know by now how grimy they are."

"I should and I do. See you at eight."

He went back to his room and finished dressing in cool whites and turned to leave the room. He was stopped by Deldee. She was dressed in a backless, strapless dress of soft clinging white that draped in gentle sympathetic folds outlining her lissome figure and hugging her breasts without a wrinkle. Her hair had been drawn back away from her face and secured back of her head by a white ribbon. She seemed frightfully young and vulnerable. His throat swelled and ached as he stood there watching her, knowing that she must have heard him on the phone.

"Señor Don, may I say something?"

"Of course!"

"Whoever she is, she can't love you as I do." Her great eyes filled slowly with tears.

"Deldee, she doesn't love me at all. She hopes to make me think so because she wishes to use me, but I know it and therefore I'm in no danger. She is no threat to you in the least."

She relaxed and her shoulders slumped. "I have no rivals, and yet—"

He laughed from sheer amused amazement. "Darling, you want the world to change overnight. You're not willing for things to crystalize in their own time."

She stepped close to him, her jaws tight and her body rigid. "But I want you now. I don't want to have to wait for time."

He reached out and drew her gently close but she resisted him, her voice coming in an agonized whisper. "Please, Don, don't kiss me again if you don't mean it. I couldn't stand it, I just couldn't stand it."

He held her for a moment, looking into her paintwisted face, the depths of her dark eyes. Then he kissed her. For a moment she was stiff, but she melted finally and her body pressed close, transmitting heat and hunger through her clothes and his until his leaping heart pounded audibly. Her lips mingled with his, parted, and her sweetly hesitant tongue met the probing search of his and the world seemed to stand still. A great wave of understanding passed through his consciousness, leaving him trembling and cold with the realization. Then he remembered his previous experiences and the wave that had washed him along receded and left him stranded in the sands of disillusionment again.

He released her gently and said, "Deldee, will you wait a little while, just a little while? Until I can collect myself?"

She sighed and nodded. "I will wait because I have to, not because I want to."

He kissed her again and then left, calling to Pepé. When he had disappeared Pepé stepped from the darkness of the hallway and said in a low voice to Deldee, "You are a fool even if you are my sister."

"What do you know about such things?" she flared hotly.

"I know enough not to rush a man who, having been bitten by women before, is fearful of teeth—even false ones. Ever since he has been in this house you have acted like a virgin mare in heat, always wanting to make him chase you over a thousand acres before you will stand for him. Thereze and Esta, I might remind you, have no such silly ideas. It would be tragic, wouldn't it, if one of them should make off with your man?"

Having delivered himself thusly, he walked on out to find Don, who had need of his car.

Soldarez met him in the hotel lobby. "Have you girded your loins and prepared for the acting stint of your life?"

Don scowled at the improbably impeccable Phil and sighed. "I'll try. If she's half as smart as women are supposed to be she'll see through it in a minute. She already thinks I sound distant."

"In that case, allow me to suggest a few stiff hookers of bourbon before you walk into her parlor. She, I might add, has been hitting the bottle with suggestive frequency for a couple of hours."

"Suggestive of what?"

"That she's pretty tightly strung. I can't imagine why. Pepé, trot up to room forty-two and inform Señora Caraway that Señor

Don has been detained but will be up presently." Pepé scuttled away.

"Lead the way and I'll get some dutch courage aboard," said Don, watching Pepé take the stairs two at a time.

Don stared at the drink the waiter put before him. "Forty millimeter guns on half tracks. That means they're expecting trouble. They're prepared for anything."

Phil nodded and sipped his drink. He lighted a long black cigarette which he allowed to hang at an angle from his lips.

"Those forties remind me that they might not like aircraft snooping around," he said. "I was questioning an old man who lives in a small valley the other side of the range and according to him a plane that sounds like a DC-6 has been coming in from the east at low altitudes to the strip at night for some time."

"So you think they're going back empty?"

"Yes, as a matter of fact, I do. I'm having the plane watched at Paraiso. They take off loaded and come back empty. They've been in operation long enough to have a considerable quantity of corium-2 ready to go. I don't know why they're tarrying unless there's some hold up in their delivery program."

"You still of the opinion they might try to deliver to Russia?"

"I am and I have reasons. That problem might be their very concern. A Russian ship in Mexican waters and unexplained might prove embarrassing. However, our good neighbor Guatemala has been playing footsie with them." He paused and his face hardened. "Now, how perfectly silly of me."

"What's that?"

"I was speaking to a colleague of mine only last night and he mentioned two strange ships that had been anchored off Quetzaltenango for three days. His coast observation spotted them, but strange ships in those waters—especially tramps—only spell bananas, usually. That is, assuming that the tramps have refrigerated holds, which they don't often." He laughed shortly. "Maybe they spell bananas this time. Or maybe they're waiting to be loaded with corium-2. The report didn't impress me—for one reason, because they're not in our waters, and also because they're—" He stopped and drummed on the table with his fingers, his lips compressed. "How would they get that stuff to those ships? It'd have to be lightered if they are expecting to be loaded where they are now. Quetzaltenango is inland and there are no good ports nearby."

"Wouldn't it have to be lightered no matter what?Surely they wouldn't depend on getting loaded at a regular port?"

"No, of course not. Down near Tapachula there's a strip, too. It was constructed during the war for heavy traffic that due to some change in plans wound up somewhere else. It'd be perfect."

They conversed steadily for nearly an hour before Don realized that he had a load on and was supposed to visit Dariel.

"Guess I'd better go up and do some acting. I feel a little more up to it now."

"Do so and let me know what you find out, discover, unearth or otherwise become acquainted with."

He had raised his hand to knock when he heard voices coming through the vent at the bottom of the door. He held his breath to listen, expecting to learn of some sinister plot, but only heard Dariel's cooing voice inviting Pepé to take off his trousers and Pepé's not so trembling refusal. "But Señora, at your request I have already taken off my shirt. If Señor Don should come in now he would flay the hide off my back and my cousin would then take what was left and feed it to the ants."

Don backed away from the door, his face blank with amazement. Was she that bad off or was she just that way all the time?

He massaged his chin for a moment and then a thought struck him. There were slatted ceiling-tofloor doors leading into a narrow gallery from all the rooms on this floor. Quite often these doors were left open, and if they weren't locked one could listen with less chance of embarrassment. He tiptoed to the end of the hall, walked out on the balcony and started counting doors. Opposite Dariel's doors he stopped and peered in. They had been swung wide to catch the cool breeze that blew gently in from the south east and the fragile curtains were stretched inward too thin to do more than obscure the interior. He could plainly see her sitting on the bed, clad in a thin white robe, the neck of which fell away from her richly swelling breasts, her legs crossed, the fine skin of her thighs aglow. Pepé stood in the middle of the room, his willowy youthful body bare to the waist, sweating somewhat from the position he found himself in, obviously not knowing quite what to do. Nevertheless, he examined her boldly.

"You like what you see, Pepé?"

"Señora, I have never seen so much beauty. I am prostrate at your feet."

"You are not, either." She giggled alcoholically. "You're distant and I don't think you love me."

"Oh, I love you more than I can say," he insisted. "But if Señor Don—"

"We'll lock the door. You wait here, Pepé, while I take a quick shower."

When she disappeared Don hissed. Pepé jumped a foot in the air, and, with two smooth strides, slipped out on the balcony.

"Oh Señor Don. You saved me just in time. I am afraid she meant to have me take off my trousers. It was not my fault. I beg you to believe that. Before I had hardly finished telling her the message she caught me and my ribs still ache." He dropped his head. "And I must admit that she kissed me, but I had nothing to do with it. I even tried to avoid it, but she was too strong for me."

Whatever resentment Don had melted away at the humor of the situation and he chuckled softly. "She is quite a woman, Pepé."

"I know that, sir. I once watched her and my cousin, about a year ago. I have never seen anything like it. But what will I do?"

"You could run."

"But that would not be the gentlemanly thing."

"Then why don't you stay?"

"You would not mind?"

"Of course not. Have fun."

"Thank you, Señor Don. I think my education might be helped much."

"I don't think there's any doubt of that. Shhh, she's coming."

Don ducked back out of sight and Pepé turned to see her step out of the shower, the thin robe doing little other than misting her outline. She was a gorgeous creature, all white and pink and gold, and Pepé stood transfixed where he stood.

She smiled at him and drank straight whiskey from a bottle on the night table. She went to the door and turned the lock. "Now, Pepé—satisfied?"

"Oh, yes. Now Señor Don cannot get in." With a boldness that belied his years he walked to her and took her in his arms having to tiptoe a little to find her lips. Her hands became active and in a second Pepé was a slim lithe godling, young and superbly proportioned. Don could hear her breath hiss inward and the answering hiss of her robe as she shrugged it aside.

She snatched Pepé into an embrace that made the watcher's back ache for the boy, but he was made of good metal and returned as good as he received. Her lovely body was restless and eager and Pepé proved that he had already done much for his education.

He slipped from her grasp and backed away, making her whimper and follow him. "Pepé, don't do this to me … " He was in her grasp again and again his teasing made her cry out with desire. With male force she dragged him to the bed and seemed in victory to go blind and mad.

Don walked away, his skin sticky with sweat and his hands trembling. He needed a drink so he went back to the bar. He found Soldarez ramrod straight and pale with anger, standing before a fat military man, obviously a general.

"Young puppy," snarled the general—a poor figure; and he knew it, standing beside the impeccable Soldarez. "Miserable officious young puppy. You murder these wonderful gentlemen's workers and have the effrontery to say they tried to run you down and shoot you. Are you so independent that you can stand the disgrace of a court martial, Captain Soldarez?"

The captain bowed coldly. "General Mendez, I know it is within your power to court martial me, but may I suggest that it will be you and not I who will suffer the disgrace?'"

"Stand at attention, insolent puppy."

"You may stand at ease, Captain Soldarez," said a calm voice at their elbows. They turned and saw the tall impressive man with the eyes of a gimlet and the aristocratic bearing with which the Dons have chilled lesser people for a thousand years.

"Your Excellency," stammered Mendez.

"Captain Soldarez is working under my express orders, General Mendez and unless you wish to be the victim of that court martial I suggest you sit down and become calmer. You're too old to fly into rages."

Mendez paled and stepped back, but Soldarez wasn't satisfied. "If I may be so bold, your Excellency, might I point out that he now knows your position in this matter and if that word gets to the proper or improper ears it might be fatal to our plans."

"I think that can be taken care of," said the tall man easily. "General Mendez, you may consider yourself under technical arrest indefinitely. During that period if you so much as think strongly of what has been said in this bar you shall be tried for treason. I promise it and I can virtually assure you the honor of a firing squad —unless, of course, you prefer hanging. Have I made myself clear?"

Mendez's face spoke eloquently the words his lips found impossible to frame.

"Now, sir," put in Phil smoothly, "may I suggest that we continue this conversation without his presence?"

One look was all that was necessary to send General Mendez scuttling into the lobby and out of their sight.

They took a protected table and Phil introduced Don. "His Excellency *el Presidente* Eduardo Tallemand, Señor Don Gerdt of Texas."

Tallemand's face relaxed in a smile as he held out his hand. "I know of you from my son who thinks there is nothing quite like a flyer. He found your picture in *Life* and saved it."

Don flushed and murmured some reply as they seated themselves.

"Don has helped me considerably, Eddy," said Phil, now that they were alone using a name that had been given him by their British comrades. "In fact, he was with me the other night when they tried to do us in."

Tallemand nodded. "Does he know everything?"

"Everything of importance. I checked him thoroughly."

"Good. Now bring me up to date."

They discussed the latest developments at some length, then Tallemand said, "Do you expect those ships to come into our waters?"

Soldarez frowned. "I must admit I'm stumped there. There's an air strip near the border of Chiapas and Guatemala that might be used. Trucked from there to some isolated spot on the coast, the . material could be lightered into the vessels. I doubt that they'd want to be caught with such a load in our waters, but all I have to go on there is conjecture."

"The main thing is to prevent them from getting away with any amount. As we agreed before, it is all right to let them process the material for us—but they musn't get away with it."

"And yet they might."

"What?"

"Eddy they're loaded to the teeth. We saw two half tracks mounting twin forties. With that stuff in evidence there's no telling what they have and how many men. I couldn't hope to stop them with the force I have."

"Then you must have a body of men in reserve. Picked men."

"You can say that again," said Don. "Picked men. You can bet theirs are picked."

"And I'd suggest four or five Mustangs," said Tallemand, "with rockets."

Don's heart leaped almost against his will. "You wouldn't have a couple of F-4Us or a Hellcat would you?"

Tallemand smiled. "Your government has been generous. Yes, I think we could find you one. They're your choice?"

"I've flown them. I never flew an F-51."

"Don, you've just come back from the wars," said Phil. "Why don't you just sit this one out?"

"Quiet! I'm so damn excited I can't sit still. I hope it's a Corsair. Brother, what a plane, and I'm the original dead eye dick with rockets. We used them a lot in Korea. Also napalm bombs, twenty millimeter guns and H. E. I can skip a bomb off the water and into a barrel."

"Braggart. Well, you might get to show what you can do. I don't believe we can stop them without a fight. They have too much at stake. One man has disappeared as legally dead and put himself in a spot to make millions, if I'm any judge."

They talked on for a few minutes; then Tallemand got up to leave. "I'm a busy man, Phil, and I'll have to get back. Keep me posted."

When he had gone Don leaned back and sighed. "Dammit, I want a drink the worst way. Work your magic, Phil."

The magic was worked and Don tossed a triple down and gruffed the slivers out of his throat.

"I meant to mention," remarked Phil, "that you looked like a man who had had a visitation when you came in."

"I watched one. I never got to see Dariel."

"Why?"

"She wouldn't let Pepé go. She wanted him the worst way, but your instruction has been such that by the time he was ready to let up on her she would have called the Army and Navy to rescue her if she'd been strong enough."

Phil chuckled. "So the estimable Pepé came through. What did you mean, my instruction?"

"He watched you a year ago when you and Dariel had fun."

Phil's dusky face grew a dull red. "Why, the nosy, impertinent little iguana."

"Yes. I think he was impressed."

"I'm covered with mortification. There are things one does in the privacy of one's boudoir that he doesn't care to have nosed about. I've a notion to skin him."

"Don't. His only reaction was one of admiration and I can assure you he used your technique beautifully—and probably got in a few licks of his own."

"That little devil. Do you know, Don, that boy is a phenomenon. I hang around their house a lot and use my uncle's stable whenever I feel in need of a ride. Pepé was bedded down in the hay with a new maid one day. She was eleven, I think, and Pepé was all of eight. Following my natural curiosity I found that being eight was no obstacle to a born artist. Imagine a child making an undergrown girl practically claw the walls down. I rather imagine she was a virgin and yet he made wild wild music ring in her ears."

"I'm afraid age doesn't mean much," said Don, his spine crinkling afresh at the memory of Pepé's lovemaking. "At Pepé's age I'd have dived out of that two story window to escape her. His main concern was that I might come in and skin him and you'd feed the remnants to the ants."

"That's not a bad idea," growled Phil, his skin growing pink again, "the spying little satyr."

"Do you think Mendez is quieted?"

"Yes, but I rather suspect interference from other levels, too. If I could blandly turn them over to Eddy and forget the matter I wouldn't mind, but the moment I invoke the highest power, my position is exposed. They'll know the jig is up and that they'll be for it"

"That'll have to happen sooner or later."

"Correct, but in my own time, I hope. For it to happen now would catch us with our pants in a precarious position."

Don sighed gustily. "My pants," he said with a sort of plaintive bitterness, "have been off so much lately that I sometimes wonder which position would be precarious for me."

Phil let go a gale of laughter that rang from the ancient ceiling and made patrons glance questioningly in his direction.

Don finished his drink and said. "I'm going back to the Hacienda del Cortez and make a manful effort to get a night's sleep."

"Well, luck, chappie and all that sort of rot."

"You do pretty good as a Hollywoodish version of General Crack," Don told him, "but as a Limey you're as phony as a lead thruppence."

CHAPTER TEN

DON WAS surprised to find Pepé at the wheel of the car as he came from the hotel. "Well, young man, what do you say for yourself?" asked Don severely.

Pepé grinned very much like his diabolical cousin. "Any words I say must in justice be spoken for the Señora. Whattawoman." He sighed ecstatically.

"Oh, I don't know," scoffed Don casually. "When I last heard she was begging you on bended knees to stop."

Pepé laughed exultantly. "Would that not be music to your ears, that your love is so strong it cannot be withstood?"

"Yes, I can see your point. Were you educated?"

"Considerably." He gunned the motor to life and pulled away from the hotel. "She became so fearful of my love and—" He shook his head. "I hardly know what to call it. She would almost have spasms every time I'd touch her. Then she contrived a way out of it."

"She did? How?"

Pepé told him in blunt simple words making him sweat anew. "You mean she did that?"

"She did, and then I was soon in her own predicament. I felt I should leap from the window if she touched me again. I think she then became a little angry because of the torture I had put her through and decided to put me through the same punishment and until I found a countermeasure I was seriously considering calling for help."

"What was the countermeasure?"

Pepé grinned again. "I did the same thing to her." Don cursed. "Why, you shameless puppy."

"Señor Don, what shame is there to that which comes naturally as in the song I once heard said?"

"Oh, hush. I've been so churned tonight I feel like butter."

He didn't know it, but he was in for further churning. He entered his room and slipped out of his coat and stripped off his tie; then he heard the noise and spun about, the .45 glinting dully in his hand. It was Deldee. The relief was so great that he dropped the gun and had to pick it up. His relief, however, was shortlived; because he saw that Deldee, stars in her eyes and a sort of hypnotic fixity on her face, was dressed in white pajamas with about the texture of a half-hearted gesture.

"Señor Don, please forgive me."

"What for, Deldee?" His throat was so dry that he avoided croaking by dint of sheer will.

She shuddered and covered her breasts with her forearms. "For coming to you like this."

Having been subjected to an endless series of shocks, Don's fall from the edge of reality was quicker this time than before and he chuckled crazily. "I'm not sore. I'm glad. You're the most unbelievably lovely woman I ever saw." He leaped forward and drew her to him in a fierce embrace, crushing her lips beneath his own. Like a dead person she went limp in his arms and allowed him to massage the skin of her back and fit her to him like a glove. When he released her, she crumpled to the floor weeping, while he stood stupidly by and didn't put out a hand to catch her.

After a while she looked up and saw him seated on the edge of the bed staring numbly at her.

"I didn't know what to do. I love you so that it's killing me and you—you—" She hung her head and her hair fell forward, obscuring her face. Tears dripped from her eyes for a while, but her head came up again. Don felt stricken with a malaise that rendered both body and mind to nothing. He felt detached, apart from reality, and yet his heart seemed about to burst from the sight of her on the floor, her legs swung over to one side, her arms folded across her stomach and her eyes begging for his love.

"So," she said in a low soft voice in which there was still a suggestion of tears, "I am a shameless woman. I come to you tonight for you to take me. Maybe when I have given you everything I have to give, maybe you can give me something. Oh, Don!" Her face twisted with pain, "I'm doing this so badly. It didn't sound that way when I thought it out." She got up and fell at his feet, hooking an arm over his knees. "Don, it took all the courage I had to come here like this. I crushed my pride, my modesty, even my morals. Please don't make me have to entice you. I don't believe I could do that."

He managed to find his voice. "Deldee, listen to me and try to understand. No enticement you could possibly think of would touch the picture you make in those pajamas. You are the most utterly, dangerously, femininely seductive creature I ever saw. But I can't do that to you. Have you ever stopped to think what you'd feel toward yourself afterward if you let me take you?"

A sigh fluttered into her throat. "Yes. I've thought about it. But if you would love me a little afterward, it wouldn't matter."

Strength surged back into his frame and some clarity returned to his brain. Phil's words came back to him, strengthening him further. "I'm especially anxious that nothing in the nature of a tragedy should strike Deldee Cortez."

He stood up and caught her by the shoulders, shuddering and nauseated at the racketing shock of his nerves as he sensed the warmth of her skin, the ghosty fragrance of her hair, the wide questioning eyes, and the slight tremor of her full ripe lips. Again he was burned by the unbelievable richness and smoothness of her olive skin, the ineffable grace of the lines of her torso as they swooped downward from her breasts to the narrow waist, blending with exotic perfection to the swells of her hips.

Something within him that had been drawn tighter and tighter, something of the tension that had been mounting in him was at long last drawn to its last ounce of resistance and parted. For a moment he looked at her with opaque, sightless eyes. Then he drew her to him gently and, holding her close wept like a tired child. She led him to the bed and sat down, drawing his head to her breast and crooning softly to him, her own tears splashing hotly on his neck.

The cleansing operation finally stormed itself out and he sat up giddily, stood and caught her arm. "It's time for you to go now, Deldee. Thanks a million. You just saved my life."

Her eyes were steady and damp. "Don. I came to give you my body and you didn't take it."

"I know. And it was the hardest job I ever tackled. Don't come again because I don't believe I could stop myself again."

Her smile was tremulous and so sweet that the fierce ache sprang into his heart again. "I don't think I could ever get up the nerve again. But tell me why, please?"

He sighed gutturally. "That's a hard question. Maybe it is because I don't want to defile a wonderful woman, the most wonderful woman I ever met Maybe—" He lifted his shoulders. "All I said could be a lie. The next time you might be sorry you came."

"I'm not sorry now."

"I know. Nothing happened this time."

"Oh Don, what a fool you are. Don't you know you just bared your soul to me?"

She sounded a bit dramatic and young, but the young are always dramatic and their drama is truth.

"I guess I did." He led her to the door and kissed her like a brother. "Good night, Deldee."

"Good night, Don. You don't have anything else to tell me?"

"Not now. I've got to get straight with myself first, but don't press me. Don't make me hint at something that might never come about."

He closed the door, walked to the bed and fell face downward, rolled over, curled up in a protective bundle and fell instantly asleep.

Dariel's summons the next morning had the peremptory ring of an order and Don, wishing to do his talking person-to-person, agreed to come up at once and have breakfast with her.

It was served in her rooms. He found her already seated, clad in a misty pink negligee that was not much more than a motion toward propriety, since the neck dropped deeply into the valley of her breasts and was held together by the rigid hillocks over which it could not climb.

"Good morning Don," she said crisply, "even though I'm not particularly well disposed toward you. Who stopped you last night? Some local piece?"

He was shocked at the change in her. He had expected her to continue on the same tack they had shared in Black Point.

"Being a woman," he retorted coolly, "you'd naturally prefer to believe that. And what if I did? Is that something you wouldn't do?"

She dropped a piece of toast and looked at him in horror. "If this is the way you're going to treat me—"

"Oh, come off it. What do you take me for, anyway?"

"I'm burt," she persisted. "After what we were to each other."

"You'll heal quickly enough—if Pepé stays around." She went pale. "What—?"

"Please Pepé," he mimicked, and dodged just in time to avoid a thrown saucer that sailed on and smashed to bits against the wall. "Do that again," he said ominously, "and I'll flog the tail off you."

She was quivering with rage. "A dirty snooper. I was a fool to leave my doors open last night."

"You're a fool in a lot of ways. Like kissing Abel before the plane even left the ground."

She smiled embarrassedly, making him marvel at her quick changes of temper. "That was a pretty silly thing to do. I wondered if you had seen."

"I saw. By the way, are you going to go on with this farce?"

"You mean of hunting for my husband?"

"Yes."

She caught her breath, then stole a guarded glance at him. "Then you know?"

"I know your husband is alive and that you knew it all the time."

"Then you know quite a lot else. How did you find out?"

"Snooping here and there. I had luck. He bought that cadaver, you know."

Her face went a little pale. "I have a proposition to make, Don."

"So I had imagined. Make it good and I'll send Pepé around to see you."

"He'll be back," she said coolly, "and you can't insult me."

"No," he said sarcastically, "I can only hurt you."

"I am also impervious to sarcasm."

"I can believe that, too. Who do you hope to be, another Eva Peron?"

"Why not? She did it. The thing is, Don, I tried to tie you down by my attraction—I do have some attraction, don't I?"

"Oh, indubitably. No one could deny that."

"But I failed by being a silly woman. Now the mask is off. We need you."

"Go on. I'm listening."

"There's a chance for you to make yourself independently wealthy just by doing something you know how to do."

He sat impassively and waited for her to continue.

"Did you ever check out in a DC-6?"

"Yes."

"How would you like to fly one for us?"

"Who is 'us'?"

"At the moment that's not of top importance. You will be paid a sum that will make your eyes bug out."

"Why? Flyers come a dime a dozen these days."

"Not the kind we want. Don, this thing is so big it will be hard for you to take it all in at first. If you come with us you'll be high in the organization because you came among the first and because I am, in a manner of speaking, your sponsor. I think you're an intelligent, resourceful man and we can use men like you."

He sat back and lit a cigarette. "I gather I'm wanted to fly DC-6s. Flying what? Where to, and how does a simple job of flying command such an awe-inspiring salary?"

"For the moment you must take my word for it. The details can come later."

"You mean after I've accepted?"

"Yes."

He shook his head. "Looking a gift horse in the mouth seems to be the alternative to buying a pig in a poke. I don't want any."

Her face was seriously composed. "But why not? What else could you do that would earn you a third of what we'll pay?"

"A number of reasons. For instance, this little conference has come about in as devious a manner as I ever saw. First the love boat business and dead husband, but now the mask comes off and I'm hired to smuggle opium out of some place to some place."

"Who said opium?"

"Just a figure of speech. Smuggling something, anyway. Opium, gold, jewels, Chinese laborers—what difference does it make? Usually when a job is paid for three times there is ten times the usual risk to the lug's neck. I like my neck, having protected it rather successfully through two wars."

"Why don't you think it over, Don? You don't have to decide now."

"Thanks. I'll do that. You might use some of that time your-self to decide to come out in the open and let me know what it is I'm to smuggle. Don doesn't put his head in the noose without knowing what for. Have you tried Phil? He's a flyer, too."

"I'm afraid Phil is a little too honest and hardheaded."

"Yeah. You tried to soften him up once, didn't you?"

Her face darkened. "I didn't think of him as one who would kiss and tell."

"He didn't. Pepé was the informant. He watched, and accord-ing to him it was a pretty warm kiss."

"Don't bother trying to make me angry about that or my other fleshly leanings, Don. I'm just a healthy girl with a super-healthy appetite. I learned long ago that to confuse libido with love was a sure road to bumps. I'll take mine straight."

He grinned without humor. "Somehow I find this new you preferable to the you I had all dreamed up, in spite of the fact that you're slightly nauseous. Do you come with the deal?"

Her smile was a light going on in a dark room. She got up, walked over to him, and planted a wet sensuous kiss on his lips that left him oddly cold. "Of course, silly. I'll need you, too."

He placed a hand over each breast and shoved her back. "Thanks, kid, but I'll take mine straight, too."

"What do you mean?"

"When I want fertilizer I like it tagged as such. Seeing it labeled as lilac toilet water always carries the possibility of shock."

He got up and started for the door and then turned. "Ta ta, kid. Let me know when you become communicative."

Her face was enigmatic, but her eyes were flint hard. "I wouldn't try so hard at insults, Don," she said softly. "You might succeed some time."

He closed the door and felt a little chill flit down his spine. He wouldn't start this tilt by being fool enough to believe her harm-less. She was *el tigre* whose claws were not absent just because they were sheathed.

As he passed through the lobby he found himself button-holed by the clerk. "Captain Soldarez asks that you join him in the bar, Señor Don."

"Thanks, Bemadino."

He walked into the bar and found Phil nursing a tall green drink. Don made a face and sat opposite him. "What's that bilious-looking thing?"

"This is a mint cooler. It is not intended for serious drinking."

"Have you seen Carol lately?"

Soldarez grinned. "I saw quite a lot of her last evening. Carol had been bitten by the dog."

"How's that?"

"She started out to pump me and found her choice of methods so diverting that she is a little overcome and inclined to become slightly tail heavy. Her trim tabs are out and her stability is a matter of chance."

Don chuckled. "One would think that fact eventually would have occurred to the powers that be—if they're not fools. I wouldn't trust a woman to do anything in your company but eagerly surrender certain intimate articles of attire."

Phil's eyebrows lifted and fell. "You overestimate me. What about your appointment this morning?"

"I was asked to join the organization and fly transport for them. A fabulous salary was suggested with a bonus, whenever I desired, in the form of Dariel."

Phil chuckled and puffed on his long cigarette. "They're loaded with attractions, wot wot? Does she include Pepé in her plans?"

"She didn't say."

"She has already started a program designed to include him in another night's fun."

"Oh? Well, I can see why. He gave her something many an older man has failed to provide. I can see where Pepé had been underestimated."

"Where is he, by the way?"

"I don't know. He wanted to drive me in this morning, but I wanted to walk some of Deldee's influence out of my system. She's getting to be a four-pronged problem. Only your remark saved what might have turned out to be a situation of the most complex order last night."

"Which remark was that?"

"The one about not wanting her to be the target of a tragedy."

The captain sighed and bored his gaze into Don's eyes, creating the uncomfortable impression that it could see what Don had so carefully left unsaid. "Don, son, why don't you relax and let things take their natural course?"

Don frowned. "Dona Maris suggested the same thing, but dammit, you both forget that if I did, the very tragedy you're afraid of might happen. You don't have to be too intelligent to see that."

Phil laughed, delightedly. "You're the transparent one, son."

"How?"

Phil leaned forward, the mirth gone suddenly from his face. "Don't you know that before you would hurt Deldee, you would do just what she's hoping you will do? Don, you're not a man to cause a tragedy."

Don was slightly offended. "You mean you'd be in favor of me taking her in the heat of passion and then, under the whip of remorse, marry her?"

Phil shrugged. "I think you're being unnecessarily brutal about it. Have you ever asked yourself just why all this concern over Deldee when it is not usually a part of your *modus operandi?*"

Don lit a cigarette and leaned back. The more Phil talked the deeper he struck into things Don had been carefully avoiding.

"Your silence," said Phil musingly, "is more eloquent than what you might have said. Think it over."

There was a short silence that might have become a long one had it not been for the ripping crack of a highpowered rifle that shattered the peace and quiet of the bar. There were screams, tipped-over chairs and the crash of glassware.

Phil, on his feet in a split second, was issuing orders in machine gun Spanish. The whiplash voice seemed to quiet the patrons who then had time to gather around the prone figure of a man not twenty feet away from the table where Don and Phil had been sitting.

"What the hell," asked Don as they looked at the man.

"The minions of evil! Pedro, come here."

A short broad man came forward. He was dressedpeon fashion in coarse white shapeless clothes, barefooted with a broad brimmed dirty sombrero.

"When did you see this?" Phil pointed to the dead man.

Pedro smiled exposing white even teeth. "He has been around for an hour. At first there were too many patrons so he waited. I waited also, behind a palm over there in the corner." As he spoke his fingers caressed the slim rifle he carried. It had mounts for telescope sights and Pedro seemed quite familiar with the piece.

Phil bent over and turned the man revealing a short barreled Webley revolver. "An international brigade. First the Schmeisser and now a Webley." A search revealed nothing by the way of identification, not even laundry marks on his cheap bargain basement clothes. His face was narrow and about all that could be said of it was that it looked foreign.

"One-man assassins," said Phil as his minions surged forward to take over, "usually means that those behind the guns are afraid to send more than one because of the possibility of getting others captured and questioned. Naturally, they suspect us of not being above their own methods of extracting information. Sometimes there is much to be said for such methods."

At this juncture Bernadino dashed into the bar. "Captain Soldarez, the telephone for you. Important."

In two minutes he was back, his face dark and hard. "Pepé just got back from the camp with some inartistic carving on his person. Shall we go to the hospital and see what it's all about?"

Don Ramon met them at the entrance of the little hospital that was set delicately in a brooch of palm and oak trees with the ubiquitous bed of lurid flowers and winding walks.

"He is not badly hurt," he explained calmly, "but he has rather an unusual story to tell."

The story was unusual, to say the least. Pepé told them, his eyes hot and burning in sharp contrast to his pale face. "I went to the camp this morning, Señor Don, when you said you'd walk, to see that things were well and to pay my respects to Señora and Señor Tazapa. While I was there men came and beat the poor Señora and struck Señor Tazapa over the head with gun butts even though he is blind and could do them no harm. Two of them forcibly took Ynez and Yma away while a third searched the brush for Yolanda, who had run away. He found her and I found him at the same instant. I spilled his bowels with one wipe of my knife, Señor Don, after the fashion of your own Marines, and he is now in hell where he should have remained when he was planted in his mother's womb by a *cabrón*. The old man and woman I brought back here because they were injured."

"I also brought Yolanda, too, because she would have been left alone." The boy raised himself on his elbow. "We must go after them—now. I beg of you to allow me to go along. I know where they are camped."

"Where?" asked Phil, his face a solid, expressionless mask.

"Up the road toward the mines. I had seen the place before, but there was no one around at the time."

Phil looked at Don. "Could that be an advance post, sort of a sentry box?"

"Could be. Your men haven't reported it?"

"They aren't operating in that area because it didn't seem necessary. Nothing was going on there, but what could have made them attack a defenseless old man and woman and steal the girls?"

"They were drunk, or nearly so," said Pepé, his lips almost blue and his face icy with hate.

Phil nodded abstractedly. "Three or four men on lonely sentry duty, probably no good for anything else, and one of them buys a jug of tequila. They had probably seen the girls." He nodded. "And it is unlikely that they've let the news filter back to those in command. That might well get them shot for jeopardizing the whole operation for the sake of a pair of women." His lips tightened. "My uncle," he said to Don Ramon, "would you favor me by calling the hotel and instructing Pedro in my name to get two men and await me there. We will question Pepé further, and then I'll pick them up."

CHAPTER ELEVEN

THE INSTANT Don Ramon's back was turned Pepé slid out of bed and jumped into his clothes. "As you can see by my actions, I am not badly injured. Only a slice along a rib. Please do not deny me this opportunity to get back at those *javelinas*."

Don looked at Phil, who shrugged. "What does the doctor say?"

Pepé sneered. "He mumbles about staying in bed a few hours. What does he know of matters of the heart?"

"I thought you dropped by to pay your respects to the old people," said Phil severely.

Pepé grinned. "That was but quick fiction with which to fool my father."

"Who," retorted Phil, "was of course not fooled any more than we were."

It was late afternoon and the Sunbeam, carryipg a full load, eased around the last curve that placed them within a quarter of a mile from the spot Pepé had identified as the possible campsite.

They pulled the car out of sight in a cedar thicket and from there proceeded on foot.

After twenty minutes of careful maneuvering they found themselves on a shelf overlooking the spot. Don was moved to whisper to Phil. "They have a good lookout spot, but it's a cinch to flank."

"Correct. I hope all their military savvy is no better than the placing of this spot—which after all might have been intended solely for quiet observation. Ah, there they are."

Pepé sucked in his breath hard and tensed like a cat ready to spring. Below them two men came into view half carrying, half dragging the still fighting Yma. Behind them came another, his hands full with Ynez. The girls were entirely nude, and though they had obviously been roughly treated they were too full of fight to have been seriously hurt.

Pedro said, "It would be easy to drop them. One shot for each."

"Give me the rifle," snarled Pepé, beside himself with rage. "I am a wonderful shot and—"

"Be quiet," rapped Phil sharply. "Your rage is understandable, but greater things are at stake. Wait, Pedro, until they are quieter. Then get one in the leg—take the one with the red hair. Luis, you concentrate on the one with the grey trousers: Tomas, you take the one wrestling with the girl alone. No mortal wounds. Just something to keep them from running."

The man holding Ynez grew tired of her feline resistance and struck her a hard blow on the jaw. As she fell he went down on top of her, his drunken laughter ringing out and his intention all too clear. Gluttonously he mouthed her sweat-streaked breasts.

"Fire, for the love of God!" screamed Pepé, unable further to remain quiet.

"Fire," came the calm voice of Phil. The three rifles cracked almost as one and three men lay scrabbling about on the hard ground like hamstrung animals.

Phil had to forcibly drag Pepé from the man who had attacked Ynez before the boy killed him, which was manifestly his intention. He sobbed jerkily as he recovered from Phil's muscular heave, pawed the girl's hair from her eyes and wiped bits of pebbles and sand from her dank skin. The men gave the girls shirts to cover as much as possible of their nakedness while Don used his belt to stop the bleeding of one man whose femoral artery had been severed.

"Search the place thoroughly," Phil barked at his men. "Put the bleeder on the floor of the car and lash the other two any place you can. Pepé, do you feel equal to walking the girls over to the camp? We'll send back for you."

Pepé, whose rage was now waning, nodded. "Let Señor Don bring back my car. We will await him at the camp."

The girls now recovered and seemed none the worse for their experience except for various abrasions and bruises. They smiled and chattered their approval of the project, hovering over Pepé and examining the bandage he proudly displayed, reminding them that he had received it in their defense.

As they prepared to leave, Pepé said to Don, "Bring Yolanda back with you if she is at my home."

"Why?" asked Don suspiciously.

Pepé winked hugely and went to join the girls who stood together at the edge of the trail, their breasts and most of their legs unashamedly exposed. Don's mouth suddenly flushed with saliva as he caught the emanations from "their hot eyes and with a hearty curse he went to the Sunbeam and squeezed in.

It was dark before they reached the valley floor and the headlights of the Sunbeam sprayed the sides of the roads as they maneuvered around sharp curves, picking out the cruel *cholla* burrs frosted with steel-like spines and the huddled shapes of boulders. The man on the floor groaned from the cutting pressure of his tourniquet, but the whistling wind drowned any sound those tied to the front fenders might have made.

Don was taken directly to the Cortez house and he strode straight to Pepé's automobile. He did not have the slightest intention of enduring the return trip with Yolanda probably plaguing him every foot of the way. But still another problem arose. Deldee, seeing him get out of the Sunbeam, came out just as he climbed into the Ford.

"Señor Don—you're leaving again?"

"Yes, Deldee. We left Pepé, Yma and Ynez up at the camp. I'm going back to pick them up. There wasn't room in Phil's car."

"Please, may I go with you?"

He hesitated, not particularly caring to have her along, but feeling that she would probably serve as a buffer between him and the other Tazapa girl—the one Pepé would choose to let sit with him.

"Is it so much to ask?" she said in a small voice that cut him so deeply he ached all over with a sudden flaming intensity. Her eyes were as soft and pleading as a puppy's and her heart throbbed in the eagerness of her face.

"Sure, kid," he said, his voice almost cracking. "You can go."

Her face lighted suddenly as though he had thrown the switch of her soul and he was conscious of a feeling of near anger because she was so absurdly pleased.

They rode along through the quiet night, neither of them speaking until at last the girl said, "Are you angry at me, Señor Don?"

"No, of course not." He grinned weakly. "At certain times you will call me Don, then you fall back on formality. Just call me Don."

Her smile was so abjectly grateful that he felt like banging his head against something hard. Her voice was feather soft. "I'll call you Don, if you don't really mind."

He compressed his lips and asked a question which was a betrayal that angered him. "Why did you want to come with me, Deldee?"

"Because I see so little of you—and because I love you. I hope you are not angry at me for coming. And for last night."

"No, I'm not angry at you." He was quite angry at himself, however, and even more so when he heard himself say, "How can you be so sure about something like this?"

She leaned back against the seat, little tremors of muscle rippling the smooth expanse of her bare stomach. "I listen to my heart, Don. I heed what it says." She turned to him. "Why don't you?"

His voice was grim. "Because my heart has been instrumental in getting my head cut off several times, three to be exact."

She sighed. "Maybe it will get mine cut off, too. Is it bad?"

"You have no idea. Bad enough to frighten one to death at the possibility of having it repeated."

The skin of her brow was unaccustomed to frowns and hers was unconvincing. "I suppose so. But I always thought that my love would be so great a thing that nothing and no one would be able to withstand it. Yet it just doesn't seem to reach you."

He let a despairing trickle of air from his lungs. "It isn't that way at all, Deldee. I've tried to explain. It doesn't mean that I'm not attracted. I am. Too much, and I'm afraid. Afraid for myself and afraid for you."

She was silent so long he thought she didn't intend answering. But then she said, "Don, I've never been hurt, but do you know something? I'd rather be hurt by every one I ever fell in love with than to miss the possibility of it being the real thing. How can one ever know? How did you know you would return from a flying mission? How did you know you'd live through two wars? There was an objective to be gained. You made what effort you could and trusted that the fates or God would bring you through. That's the way I feel. I might get hurt, as you say, but I'll have the comfort of knowing I did what I could. I can't make you love me and I know that. All I can do is love you with every sense I possess and hope it reaches you in a manner that will impress you and awaken any feeling you might have for me."

It was a rather long breathless speech for her and it left him feeling as though some vital wire had been disconnected. Her philosophy was strong and had such battering logical appeal that he had a feeling he was the veriest dilettante in the scheme of life and that she was the one who had the only courageous productive outlook.

"I'm sorry," he said tightly, "but there are ways things can be presented which are unanswerable. You just did it. You're right, of course. Not a single point could be argued. But still … "

"I know," she said, "I've read about people like you."

He glanced at her sharply. "What do you mean?"

She sighed. "What does it matter?" She shrank up in her corner and remained silent all the way to the camp.

Pepé and the girls came out looking chipper but disheveled, which made Don wonder afresh at the energy and bounce of youth. Already the past hectic week was beginning to wear him thin in spots.

Pepé was surprisingly well-behaved on the trip back to the village; whether it was from exhaustion, which he doubted, or the presence of Deldee, which he more than suspected, Don could not be certain.

At the barracks where Don went after he put the others out there was something like a well-ordered stir. Captain Soldarez walked around briskly, giving orders that were carried out at a fast trot. Arms were being inspected and ammunition crammed into belts that would be crossed on men's chests. Boxes of hand grenades were pried open and ready. Small mortars were being cleaned and oiled and ammunition for them stacked. Machine guns were emerging from their grease, and Don noted several makes. Vickers, Browning, Thompson sub-machine guns and even the M50 Reising guns.

He tapped Phil on the shoulder. "Don't tell me you keep an arsenal like this here all the time?"

"No. It came by truck today. I have three companies of good men camped not far away, but they will remain hidden until needed. Then they'll dash by here and get equipped. They already have their rifles and a number of light machine guns. I wish I had about four batteries of 105s."

"Damn, you really expect trouble."

Phil shrugged. "In the absence of any knowledge of their strength, I'd rather be overweight than a soap bubble. If I flub this deal I might as well apply to the RAF for my old commission. And I like this place."

"Seen Carol?"

Phil gave him a peculiar glance. "No. Why?"

"Have you questioned the prisoners?"

"No."

"Then I'd watch her if I were you."

"You sound as though you knew she had asked to see them."

Don stared. "Well, I'd watch her twice as closely. What excuse did she give for wanting to see them?"

"Said she spoke several languages and might be able to help me."

"You speak enough languages to question them. I'd bet your Hungarian will work."

"My Hungarian is worse than your Spanish, but I'll keep a watch on her."

"Do better than that. Don't be here when she comes and leave orders that she be shaken down from scalp to toenails."

"That's an idea. You found the kids all right?"

"Yes, and unless I'm mistaken, Pepé had been at it again."

Phil whistled. "I can see that should I die in battle, all will be well as long as Pepé is around."

Oddly enough, Dariel appeared and asked to see the prisoners just as they were leaving the barracks-jail, but this time she found a new and unexpected Phil, whose face was stiff and uncompromising, whose eyes were hard as agates.

"It pains me to say this, Dariel," he said swiftly and not without harshness, "but you will not be able to see the prisoners. Why should you be interested?"

She was dressed in cool blue print cut square across the shoulders and neck. The daring dip between her breasts rose and fell easily with her breathing. "Just woman's curiosity, Phil. Surely you don't mind."

"I do mind very much. As of now, Dariel, you're under hotel arrest. You will return there and you won't leave unless I give permission. And I won't. You needn't look so innocent. Don and I saw you get out of the Cessna yesterday. We know all about you and your husband's activities and we're prepared to stop them. We know why you wanted Don to fly for you but he'll be flying for us. Your DC-6 won't get very far and will probably come down in flames unless it follows orders."

Her face went icy white and Don thought she'd faint. "You … know … "

"Of course. You, my dear, are in Mexico, and doubtless you and your friends thought you had bought yourself protection. You had—as far as it went. It didn't go far enough. I'd advise you to return to your hotel immediately."

She left, but if she had overestimated the power of bribe money, Soldarez in turn underestimated the mentality of Dariel Caraway. She entered her little rented coupe and headed toward the hotel while Phil casually detailed three men to watch all entrances; but as this was going on Dariel was racing up the slopes toward the crest of the range, without having stopped at the hotel. When Soldarez heard about it, he dispatched the three men detailed to watch the hotel after her in a jeep, but with little hope that they would catch her. With a sigh of mingled rage and frustration he suggested drinks in the cool of the hotel bar which Don accepted.

Two hours later Pedro who seemed to occupy the position of an incognito major stopped at their table and saluted.

"The woman is back, Captain."

"What? You caught her?"

"She nearly got away, but a flat tire spelled the difference. We had to fight our way out."

Phil made an impatient gesture. "Tell me."

"We had seen her struggling with the tire at some distance and had increased our speed, but someone else must have also seen her and realized what a position she was in. There was a rifle duel at long range and we wounded three or four. They do not know how to use cover against a marksman and I shot one through an arm and one through a shoulder."

"That's good. Place the woman in her room and station a guard at her door and one on the balcony."

"It has been done, Captain."

"You have done well. Tell the bar man to serve you tequila, as much as you desire. But I'll have your hide if I need you and find you drunk."

Pedro bowed and made his way to the bar with an air of triumph.

"Well," began Phil, massaging the palms of his hands together, "I think war will be declared shortly."

Don nodded. "They know now that something is amiss. They'll know about the captured sentries and won't know that they have refused to talk. They know Dariel tried to escape and must have a reason."

Phil tasted his drink and nodded agreement. "I'm prepared to intercept any attempt of theirs to find out what she knows. It wouldn't be unusual if they tried to get her away."

Telecos was quiet in the small hours of the dawn. At that hour even crickets and other insects were quiet and dogs had sought the sanctuary of doorsteps and slept. An occasional cock could be heard, but even they sounded sleepy.

The single policeman who patrolled the east side of the canyon sharing duties with another whose beat was the west side did not see the man who swiftly leaped from the shadow of an alley, and the sap fell with precision and force upon the back of his neck.

The clerk at the hotel was frankly asleep, his head pillowed on his arms back of the desk; he scarcely moved when the shot-loaded leather smacked into the back of his head.

Pedro Sanchez had not gotten drunk but he had fallen into the trap of slumber; he too never felt the blow that put him in a deeper sleep.

To describe the furor that arose at daylight could only be something short of just what happened. Men and women, knowing only that several people had been found bound and gagged and that Bemadino had been suffocated by his gag, were on the verge of panic. Only the clarion voice and overpowering personality of Soldarez quieted what might have had serious consequences.

Don, routed from bed by an excited Pepé, joined Soldarez in the plaza as the clamor was dying down.

"What's all this about?" demanded Don.

"I was a fool," snarled Phil, beside himself with rage. "They gagged Bernardino too well and he smothered. That does it. I'm going to pull the place apart. By the way. Your Corsair is three miles out on the government strip and I want you to make a good reconaissance. Try to talk to them on the radio and tell them to come out of there without a single weapon in the name of the Mexican Government or said Government will blast them out. Use your own judgment. Pepé'll run you out."

Pepé's eyes bugged out and he tugged at Don's sleeve. "Let us go, Señor Don, before my cousin changes his mind."

CHAPTER TWELVE

D ON, HIS 'CHUTE strapped on and his eyes narrowed against the slipstream from the three bladed prop, waved to Pepé who stood on one wing half beside himself with excitement. "She's warmed up, Pepé. Beat it."

"Please, Señor Don, can't I go along?"

Don shook his head. "You couldn't squeeze in here." Or could he? Pepé might be of help since he knew the terrain so much better than did Don. He nodded. "Okay, come in and make yourself as small as possible." Pepé climbed in, his face white with fright, but his eyes blazing with triumph and excitement.

Don taxied down to the far end of the strip, his own armpits wet with the sweat of nervous excitement. Pepé was unashamedly trembling but he was eager.

Don leaned the mixture to take off, glanced at the pitch of his prop and fed the big Pratt and Whitney all its twenty-two hundred horses could eat; the deafening roar of the surging power battered at them as he slid the canopy home. Like the gull whose wings it resembled, the fleet craft took to the air and Don yanked Her up in a hairpin turn and headed straight for the mountain peaks. In minutes he was over the camp site and a few more saw him looking down on a mining layout that had taken time, effort and much money to erect.

"Is that the area, Pepé?" asked Don, dropping a wing to give the boy a look.

He nodded. "You can see where the little railroad comes from the works and goes through the tunnel—Señor Don, look at the big planes!"

He looked and there were three DC-3s and one DC-6 drawn up close to the tunnel. He throttled back and put his earphones into place. With a forefinger he pressed the mike against his larnyx.

"F4U 100020, Mexican Army, calling mine area, over."

Four times he repeated before he heard a scratching in the earphones. "Mine to Corsair, we are reading you. What do you want?"

"You will, under the order of the Mexican Government, cease operations at once. You will marshall all your men unarmed and be prepared on instant's notice to turn them and yourselves over to the authority of the Mexican Army. You will order the planes on the strip to remain as they are or be shot down. That is all, over."

"That's not half all, bucko," snarled a new voice in his ears. "Come and get us."

"Thanks," said Don crisply. "I'll do just that." He dropped a wing, kicked hard left rudder and went into a steep dive, the stout plane whistling its peculiar song, the motor rising from its throaty bellow higher and higher in pitch.

"*Madre de Dios,*" screamed Pepé, wild with excitement. "We're going in on them!"

Don nodded, reached for the stick triggers and fingered them lightly. Down, down they went until the ground swam up at them dizzily, but he held the radio shack in his sights and poured twenty millimeter shells.into it until its entire metal surface was a smoking, holepocked mass.

They pulled out, rocketed back into the blue with Pepé screaming at the top of his voice from frenzied excitement. "Scratch one! Go get 'em again."

Don shook his head. "Not—uh oh. Look at the DC-6."

It had all four engines going and was moving slowly down the strip, picking up speed. The strip was long enough so that it could take off down wind and didn't need to lose time by taxiing.

"Corsair to DC-6, Corsair to DC-6, kill engines and come to a dead stop or I'll gut you. This is the only warning."

The plane still picked up speed so down they went again, the Corsair whistling under the force of the great engine whose bellow was rising to a scream. Don held the plane as steadily as though it were sliding down a chute and tripped his guns. The explosive slugs ripped into the big tail surface. Suddenly the plane went out of control and slewed around in a sharp circle, digging a wing into the hard surface of the strip. It came to a stop just short of the boulder defined boundary.

"Scratch two! The other two are moving, Señor Don. Go get them!"

"Corsair to DC-3s, Corsair to DC-3s, kill engines immediately or I'll blow you apart."

Suddenly the air around them became pocked with shell bursts and the Corsair bucked like a frightened horse. Don dived behind the protection, of a crag and made a wide curve back toward the planes at an altitude too low for the anti-aircraft guns to track them. The planes had stopped, however, and one even turned around and started back towards its place near the tunnel. It took a burst of gunfire just past their noses to turn the other two around. Then Don yanked the Corsair in a tight climbing turn. Then tilting the nose down, jammed the throttle to its limit and bore down on Telecos like a bolt of lightening. With a soul-shattering roar he flashed over the town and pulled up in a twisting Immelmann turn. "Hey, Phil—you listening? over."

"Barracks to Corsair. Not very well after that pass. Be a little formal, won't you. I might be recording this, over."

"Nuts. War's started. I'll have to keep an eye on those transports to see that they don't get away. They say you'll have to blast them out, over."

"It'll be a pleasure. Hold a cover on those planes and as soon as I get things rolling I'll take over in the F-51. By the way, what did you do with Pepé?"

"Oh, he's here with me getting his first lesson in strafing the ungodly. He's fine."

"How dumb can you get? See ya, fella."

Until noon Pepé and Don cruised in wide circles, careful not to get within anti-aircraft range, watching the three undamaged transports and the beetle forms of trucks crawling up the mountain side. It was one o'clock when the swell-bellied outline of the F-51 slipped by them and made a wide circle over the area, followed by the black puffs of flak.

"Mustang to Corsair. Are you reading me, over."

"Like Ned in the primer. Can we go eat now? I still have my belly tank to go on so I can stay a while yet, over."

"Take it away. I'll hold on. I hope to sew up that tunnel entrance. Say, didn't you say you were a skip bombing expert?"

"Righto. Want me to bullseye the hole?"

"Right. Go on back and pick up a five hundred pounder. That ought to do it. Drop your belly tank and gas up the wing tanks."

"Roger and out."

In an hour they were back, Pepé adamantly refusing to be left behind, demanding to see the technique of skip bombing since he intended to be a flyer some day and would be that much ahead of his fellow students.

"Watch your eye teeth," said Don. They nosed over, went into a shallow dive and hurtled straight at the face of the cliff, getting lower and lower as they grew closer. When Don tripped the bomb release they were traveling at four hundred miles an hour. With a wrench that almost dislocated their necks the gullwinged plane whipped over on one wing in a climbing turn, the reverberations of the engine bounding off the cliff with a terrific roar. They leveled out at three thousand feet just as Phil's cheer came through the earphones. "Bullseye! They're locked in now. That thing must have skated on the railroad halfway through before detonating."

Smoke and dust drifted from the mouth of the ruined tunnel as they looked. Converging on the three undamaged transports they could see three armoured cars followed by foot soldiers at a dead run.

"Now we can go eat, Pepé," grinned Don as he eased the throttle back and started the long glide toward the valley strip.

Pepé wiped his face with trembling hands. "I shall be undisputed king of the younger people," he said with satisfaction. "I, at the age of fifteen, have fought in a war and I know all about skip bombing."

At dinner that night Don apologized to Don Ramon. "I shouldn't have taken him, but I think if you'd seen him fairly dancing on that wing you'd understand."

Don Ramon laughed. "I understand perfectly. Have I not been the target of blandishments these many years? I must confess the news gave me concern, but Felipe gave me to understand that you are an excellent pilot. Still, those things give me some fear. As they used to say in San Antonio, I'd go up if I could keep one foot on the ground."

Pepé was nowhere to be seen. Don was grateful for that because at the moment what he wanted most was peace and quiet. At seven, a rather drawn Phil rolled up to the Cortez home in the Sunbeam.

"Come down to the barracks with me. Carol has been apprehended trying to give poison to the prisoners."

"I figured something like that. She had it hidden on her?"

"Correct, and it was well that I had a matron there to examine her."

"Taped to the skin, I suppose." The car ground out of the drive onto the street and Phil grinned.

"Hidden better than that. I must remember to give the matron a raise. It took four women to hold her while the matron made the examination. But sure enough, there it was."

Don compressed his lips and spat out into the gathering dusk. "Only a highly trained woman would utilize that hiding place. She'd had it, boy."

"Yes. I wonder what she'll have to say for herself?"

"How's the battle going?"

"Very well. They've been holed up now and squeezed into the mine area proper, but as I feared they're loaded with top notch ordnance. They have more forties and some old thirty-seven millimeter anti-tank guns that made hash of one of my armored cars. The driver, the fool, must have thought he was driving a General Patton tank."

"I applaud your lack of rushing tactics. We can afford to wait and there's no need to waste men."

Phil nodded and pulled the car to a stop before the barracks. "I left orders to advance only when they could safely do so and had a decent place spotted to take cover. It'll take a day or two."

"Just a minute before we get out. I don't get this deal at all. What made Caraway think he could get away with it?"

Phil shrugged. "Who knows? My guess is he had done too much business in Mexico and, like a lot of half-smart people, he thought he knew the Mexican mind too well. He bought a lot of genuflection and bribed a host of petty officials. I guess he thought he was better than he is and then, of course, he couldn't have known he'd lock horns with me."

"Go ahead and brag, but I agree on both counts. He couldn't have expected a genius in the position of a small town police official attached to the Army."

"You overwhelm me," smirked Phil, who was not in the least overwhelmed. "Let us go question the good Carol."

She was scratched, disheveled and generally out of sorts with the world, revealing in this state of mind a vocabulary that would have paled the face of a grenadier. "I want to know the meaning of this! By whose orders was I arrested and subjected to—to—" She mentioned an indignity that would have melted any linotype machine in the world.

Phil was his piratical best, his arms folded, the satanic smile on his face, teetering up and down on the balls of his feet. "Why, my dear Carol, by my orders, naturally."

"Then naturally you're—" And she proceeded to tell him in great and vehement detail just what he was and his antecedents back to the age of mud and straw.

"The fact of the matter is, dear Carol," said Phil easily, "that you were a diverting plaything for a while, but you're a bit on the thick side for intrigue. So thick, in fact, that Don here predicted what you'd do and he saw you only once. Now, who are you working for?"

"You just try to find out," she snarled, hurling another and unusable epithet. Then she turned on Don and gave him a broadside, a twin of the one she had launched at Phil.

Phil made a motion to the husky matron who had lost her temper long ago and was consequently rougher than necessary, almost hurling the girl into a bare, earthfloored cell.

"What'll you do with her?" asked Don.

Phil massaged his face with his long fingers while a devilish light gradually grew in his eyes. "I think I have an idea," he said gently, then shrugged. "We'll see. I may not need her after all."

The mine area was taken the next day without air cover. Due to the zeal with which the final assault was carried out the unexpected happened. All troops, feeling that they had everyone hopelessly bottled up in the area, left the planes unguarded and one of the DC-3s took off just as the last machine gun nest was wiped out with hand grenades.

Phil reacted unexpectedly. He lost his calm and raged mightily for fifteen minutes. Then he calmed down and apologized to the pale-faced line officer who had been in command of the attack.

"I'm sorry I lost my temper, but I still think you're a goddamned butter-brained fool. Take my compliments and your men back to your commander and tell him I say you did a sterling job. Tell him also that he hands out commissions to asses. No, don't tell him that. I'll write you a letter of commendation.

I'll add enough kudos to get you a captaincy. I'm not responsible for all the fools in the Mexican Army and I can't houseclean it. Come, Don. Let's get a drink. I need to talk strategy with you."

After they had been seated and drinks served Phil massaged his moustache cruelly. "There's hell to pay," he growled savagely.

"Of what particular brand?"

"First, there's no corium-2 at the mine. It's gone. While we were waiting for them to air lift it out they used a road everyone knew about but never thought of as a possible outlet because a burro would have trouble navigating it without breaking a leg. But just leave it to Yankee ingenuity.

"Caraway had three bull dozers working at night. The thing is as smooth as a national highway now. Trucked out at night while I had been paying three men out of my pocket to watch the air strip. Of course, they went to sleep every night, feeling, not unreasonably, that a plane taking off or landing would wake them. Sometimes I think I'm an ass.

"You can't think of everything. Where do you think it is now?"

"Think? Ye gods man, I know."

"Where?"

"Aboard those ships I told you about. They've been lightering the stuff at night, then pulling back into Guatemalan waters in the morning. As soon as Caraway gets aboard there'll go—oh hell, maybe twenty or thirty million dollars worth of the stuff."

"On just two ships?"

"Maybe more. I don't know. All I know is that the stuff is so valuable that it cuts down on the production time of plutonium production something like sixty percent and what they have will go a long way."

"Well, we have what's left."

"Yeah, what's left. And look what's left of Felipe Juan Jesus Proventud Soldarez' reputation for being a slick patootie."

They were silent for a long time, then Don's head came up—and with it came the head of Soldarez, the same light glittering in the eyes of both.

"Jeepers," said Don breathlessly.

"*Sangre de Christo*," breathed Phil ecstatically.

In the early morning light the Pacific Ocean glittered below, an immense waste of intense blue that glittered with trillions of diamonds. At twenty-five thousand feet two slim deadly aircraft droned steadily out to sea, their wings locked in close formation.

Where the cockade of Mexico once might have been seen were still wet blobs of plain gray paint; underneath their bellies the early sun glinted redly on the blunt noses of five hundred pound demolition bombs.

Don's ears caught the power hum, then Phil's voice came though. "On your port wing Don, at ninety degrees. Looks like the ducks."

"Got you," said Don exultantly. Like two birds on a string they banked and turned in unison.

"I'll go first," said Phil, "since you're better at this that I am. If I miss you get 'em."

"Roger. I'll be behind you. You sure they're the ones?"

"Dead sure. See those white crosses on black hatch covers?"

"Yeah."

"That's their identification. If I'm right, all's well. If wrong we're a coupla blinkin' pirates." Suddenly the Mustang seemed to drop away from him and went down in a sharp dive.

"Throttle back, Phil," yelled Don. "You're going too fast."

He couldn't tell whether he had been heard, but now he could see that they were the right ships. Flak blossomed out in angry black mushrooms all around the Mustang, but it went on through and continued its dive. It pulled out and rocketed back into the blue, the parent of two clear misses, too far away to be called near misses. Then Don went in, carefully and at low throttle. He fastened one of the ships in his sights, but flak explosions bucked him away the first time. He came back on. Down, down he went until even at low throttle the wings of the Corsair were screaming through the air. He yanked the bomb release, pulled out flat, and headed directly for the other one, sensing rather than hearing the dull boom behind him. At five hundred miles an hour he screamed at the ship and at the instant of releasing the bomb pulled up and over her and corkscrewed back into the blue to dodge the flak that had grown intense.

A string of excited Spanish poured through the earphones, but he ignored it until he could glance below. The first ship already had settled noticably by the stem, his bomb having gone through the after hatch and practically torn the bottom from her. The other ship had lost way and smoke and flame poured from her starboard Plimsoll line where Don had skipped a bomb into her just opposite the wheel house.

"Oh, brother," exulted Phil over his radio. "Skip bombing in the water. Where'd you learn that?"

"Saipan," said Don as he wiped the bitter sweat of nervousness from his face. It was always like this. He'd force coolness until an attack was over, then he'd go weak and the perspiration would begin to flow.

"What now?" asked Don.

"It's taken care of, practically. I'll radio the nearest vessel—ours, of course—and have them come out and pick up the survivors. They should make an interesting collection."

They sat in the hotel bar and sipped drinks. Phil's face was in a continual smile. "All's well, son, and the birds are back in their hangers with Mexico's proud emblem now visible and all vestiges of water paint gone. The prisoners are now in the proper hands and all will now be up to the courts. Naturally, our part in this morning will be a great mystery. I think the attitude of all concerned will be that whoever dropped the bombs did the world a signal service."

Don nodded. "All's over and well for you and Mexico, but here I am with my salary cut off and the prospect of diving back into the world of commerce chills me.

"How does the prospect of leaving Deldee affect you?"

Don had apparently been leaving that prospect as far back in his mind as he could subconsciously shove it, because Phil's words drove a spike deep in his vitals. "Oh, what the hell did you have to bring that up for? I'll leave for Texas tomorrow and she'll forget me in time."

"Of course," murmured Phil easily. "Women do that without too much trouble."

There was a momentary silence while Don brooded over his drink and Phil hummed an airy tune.

Don raised his head. "What did you say?"

"I beg your pardon?"

"I asked you what you said."

"When?"

"A moment ago."

"Oh. Hummm, let me see. Oh! I said women forget things easily. I think that's what I said. Why?"

"Er … nothing. I … nothing." He clamped his jaws shut hard. "I guess I'll go get my stuff ready."

CHAPTER THIRTEEN

A T ELEVEN o'clock the next morning, Phil called for Don and found a bleary-eyed, miserable man. He promptly carted him away to the hotel where he plied him with a pungent and bitter mixture, the mysteries of which Phil would not reveal. By noon Don was able to eat a great slab of pink roast beef with gravy and hashed brown potatoes, two large tomatoes, half a head of lettuce and two tall glasses of milk.

"I thought," said Phil as he lit a black cigarette, "that you were going home."

"As soon as I get packed," mumbled Don thickly. He was feeling in the pink physically, but his mind was partially blank, no little portion of which was due to his own efforts to avoid thinking.

"How long does that take?" asked Phil inexorably.

"What the hell! You trying to rush me?"

Phil shrugged lightly. "The last report I had from you, you were in a rush. Why all the sloth?"

"I can sloth all I want to," retorted Don pettishly.

Phil started laughing, silently at first, then his shoulders started shaking and it became softly vocal.

"What's so hot damned funny?" snarled Don.

"You. You're a scream. Were it not unmannerly I would scream." His mood changed swiftly. "You make me so damn mad I could kick you all the way to Laredo, Don."

Don, who was suffering the pangs of indecision, flogged emotions, hurt, and several other unidentifiable maladies in which pride played a nebulous but potent part, looked miserably toward the bar. "I think I want to get drunk."

"Why?"

"Because it is a state of being where I can regulate my thoughts. Then I don't think at all. So I want to get drunk."

"I know several well-worn clichés regarding that attitude. If you desire I'll repeat them for you."

"If there's anything I don't want to hear it is clichés of whatever sort."

"I know. You want Santa Claus to come down the chimney and make you a gift of a ready made decision." He got up. "Don, you used to be fun. You used to be an interesting guy to talk to. Right now you're boring the pants off me. Why in the hell don't you go home? Good day."

Don felt as though his last friend had deserted him. He felt very much like weeping and beating the table with his fists. Instead, he called to the nearest waiter.

Señor?"

"Bring me a pitcher of ice water with ice in it. Bring me a bottle of Country Club Bourbon and bring two glasses. Put it all on the table here and leave me alone. Get it?"

"Sí, Señor." The man bowed equably and turned away. When he had gone Don had the impulse to call the waiter back and ask him to sit and talk. The wave of loneliness was like a great boil festering in his breast and he clenched his hands until they ached and were slick with sweat.

The drinks came and he started on a marathon that came to an end when Deldee walked in and stood looking down at him. He was not drunk but in a detached state in which his mind was a delightful blank. The sight of her standing there in a green and white striped cotton dress, sleeveless and cut low at the neck, almost burst his suddenly activated thought processes as they began to rush in all directions through his head.

"Señor Don, won't you come home with me?"

He wet his lips and strove to think of some negative back chat, but it wouldn't come. Finally he nodded, got up and almost fell. She caught his arm and balanced him and led him outside to put him in Pepé's car. He didn't even remember when she got in, but eons later without remembering a foot of the journey he opened his eyes and stared out of the windshield of the car into the dense grove of cedars that shaded the front of the mountain camp.

He turned to her and found her watching him, her face calm and her eyes deeply mysterious. "Why did we come here?" he croaked, his throat as dry as dust

"I thought it would be a good place to sober you up."

He looked at her sharply, but she was serious. He got out with comparative steadiness and opened the door for her. Together they turned and went into the camp living room where Deldee lighted several oil lamps against the gathering darkness. The ruddy glow of the lamps permeated the cozy room which seemed unaccountably chilly. Deldee felt the chill too and lit the huge pile of wood that lay prepared in the cold fireplace.

Don had taken a chair near the fireplace and now sat staring into the flickering flames, his mind chaotic and entirely out of hand. After she had the fire going she went around and turned out the lamps and came to the fireplace where she dropped to her knees and sat on the thick white woolen rug. She drew her legs beneath her, folded her hands in her lap and stared at the flames also. For a long time they sat and stared in a state of semi-hypnosis, neither uttering a word. Then she slid over close to him and, hooking her arms over his legs, rested her head on his knees.

The fire played extravagantly with the lubricious sheen of her hair, making penumbras of red come and go; and to his nostrils came that ever-present fragrance that her hair always seemed to emanate. He touched its shiny surface with a gentle hand and felt the ripple of reaction as it fled through her body. From his higher position he could see the raptuous lift of her breasts illuminated through the cloth by the fire with ghostly radiance. Without knowing why he felt the sting of tears on his lids. They tumbled down his cheeks and splashed on the back of her neck, making her start and look up at him. When she spoke, her voice was so soft, so shot through with the depth and wonder of her love that he went a little mad.

"Oh Don, why do you fight it so? What is it that makes you this way? Is it because I'm Mexican? Can't I be Mexican and attractive—and human?"

The anguish of his soul flamed out at last finding its voice. "Oh my God, Deldee, don't say such a thing!" He caught her roughly by the shoulders and lifted her into his lap, cradled her head in the crook of his left arm and kissed her as he had never kissed a woman before in his life.

Sobs started from her chest but they could find no egress. She withdrew a moment to gulp for air, her eyes swimming with tears and her throat working with unspoken words. Finally she spoke. "Oh, Don, don't you see? Don't you see what it can be like?"

He didn't answer but kissed her again, listening to the shuddering spasmodic reaction of her diaphragm, as her emotions seemed almost more than she could contain. He transferred his kisses to the column of her throat which arched slightly to aid him and from there to the plane of her chest where the rises of her breasts started in rich exciting elevation.

She whimpered and cried a little as the shock of his advances contracted her muscles. With a quick performance of his hands the dress front came open and they were his for the feasting, the touch and the exalted wonder that any woman could be so beautiful.

He caught her roughly to him and kissed her lips, holding them and tasting the tender skin with his tongue, finally enticing her tongue out of hiding and when they touched, it seemed that some gigantic switch had been thrown, knotting their skins with reactive muscle, their heads swimming with overpowering rapture. His hand touched a satiny surface, an act which made her cry out and withdraw her lips to look deep into his eyes, her own blank with a sort of hypnotic wonder and a question that she had not asked. "Don—" She whimpered and wormed closer to him, resting her hand on his as it lay inactive halfway up her thigh. "Don, do you love me?"

His throat went dry and seemed to close up. "Don't ask me that," he said in a distracted voice. "Don't ask me that." He leaped to his feet, almost spilling her on the floor. "Deldee, let's go."

"No, Don. I won't go. This is now or never. I've tried every other way I know. This is the last thing I can think of. Please don't take this away from me—from us."

With a sound like an animal in pain he fell to his knees before her, holding her close and resting his face in the softness of her stomach while titanic charges of emotion ravaged his being both physically and mentally. The maelestrom of his mind could hardly have been called thought. He was only conscious of one thing, that in his arms he held the ultimate, soft, fragrant, eager, appallingly beautiful woman whose own emotions and desires were as rampant as his own.

Deldee raised her head, breathed deeply and took his face between her hands. "Don … my darling … my dearest. Take me as a man should take a woman. Love me as I was meant to be loved. Teach me the things I should know … " A sob wracked her. "For I am very ignorant. Please be gentle with me and … " Again came the sob. "I'm yours for all time but … " Her eyes filled with tears and her face twisted as she sobbed forth her plea. "Please be kind to me and if I don't … I mean … if I seem … ignorant … don't be angry with me … because … Oh, Don … I love you so … " She crumpled forward against him and sobbed bitterly, his own tears mingling with hers.

He went into her arms' embrace, his mind reeling from the touch of her body, the close rich smell of a clean healthy woman in whom the mating urge was rampant. He kissed her long and passionately, feeling the response of a novice now at the threshold of her first experience, yet eager and ripe with the knowledge of the ages.

And later, but only a little later, he remembered hearing her cry, *"Madre de Dios. Muy muchos gracias, Madre de Divs."*

CHAPTER FOURTEEN

ON THE way back Deldee was so dreamily happy that she only clung to her man's arm and lived in a world of half twilight, a world of joy no mortal can ever know who has not ascended to the heights and breathed the sting of the cold pure air of the upper stratas.

Don, on the other hand, was a trembling fearful wreck of remorse. He fell victim to a hard chill which seemed determined to shake him to pieces and reduce him to gibbering insanity.

Deldee might have noticed his condition had she not been in such a rosy haze of repleteness. When they got to the house she reacted enough to reflect that his goodnight kiss was something less than it might have been, but she was in a floodtide of optimism.

Feverishly he threw his clothes and effects into his bags and, after waiting for some time and drinking what was left in a bottle of whiskey, he stole from the house and walked to town where he spent a miserable night in the ratty little bus station until dawn began to break. He was a great numb, aching void, a void that opened fitfully for scatterings of half-formed coherences to seep through, none of which could be arranged in sequence. Then came his visitors.

First was the little priest, a mousy dried little man in a long black clerical habit, his hair sparse and colorless, his face pointed and hairless. But his eyes were ferret bright and black as currants.

"Good morning, Señor Don," he said softly.

Don merely looked at him.

"You are leaving?"

"Yes." He started at the sound of his own voice.

The little man clasped his hands before him. "I had hoped you wouldn't."

Don stared at him as though he spoke a foreign tongue.

"I really had. Wouldn't it be better if you stayed and did the honorable thing?"

"What is honor?" he rasped.

"Honor is a Holy Grail, and every man has one. It is either bright and glittering or it is dull and tarnished. It is the thing that makes him bear up when he sees another excel at a sport or a business or a skill. Honor is not bought, nor is it acquired by diligent practice. The honor of a *mestizo* is as bright as the honor of a king or potentate. It is yours and you are the only one who can soil it."

"Very pretty speech," said Don dully.

"Thank you, Señor Don. It was nice talking with you." The little man shuffled off, leaving a queer vacuum where he had stood. Don had to quell the impulse to scream for him to come back and talk more. He had become all braced for that obstinate pain in which a man will wallow when being taken to task, but it fell flat and it was not used. A blaze of anger licked at him, making him stand up, his fists clenched and ready to fight. But the only thing to fight was a poor old peon woman who shuffled by with a bunch of bananas perched precariously on her head.

It was only fifteen minutes till bus time when the Sunbeam hissed richly up to the stone curb and the immaculate figure of Captain Soldarez stepped out, balanced like a dancer, debonair and lacking only his smile. His face was a block of carved teak and his eyes blank bits of onyx. He stood there tapping the top of a brilliant boot with his little rawhide swagger stick.

Finally Don could stand it no longer and snarled. "All right, dammit, say it."

Again the long fixed stare and a gradually visible sneer on the handsome lips. Then the teeth showed whitely in a diabolical smile. "I should soil my wonderful mouth?" He turned and entered the Sunbeam and drove away without another look.

Don shot to his feet and looked wildly about, but again he could see nothing with which to fight. The rattle of the dusty bus as it pulled up to the curb, took his attention. He jerked his luggage off the bench and fled to the interior of the bus; the driver looked at him curiously.

He huddled in a seat so near unconsciousness that he hardly knew when they pulled away from the village and bumped toward the notch in the mountain range.

He was leaving. He tried to pummel into being some sort of joyous reaction from the fact, but failed.

He was leaving. Leaving Deldee and Yma and Yolanda and Ynez and Esta and Thereze. Leaving…

Felipe Soldarez was driving like a maniac along the twisting mountain road that led to the mines, something he rarely did, having the proper respect for life and property and considerably more than that for his own life and property. Suddenly he slid the fleet car about in a little clearing and headed back to the village, slumped a little, with some of the hardness gone from his face. When he arrived in town he went directly to the house of Don Ramon Cortez where he tried to find some member of the family, but no one seemed about. Then he saw Deldee coming up the drive with a black shawl over head, barefooted, the personification of some tragic virgin of a hundred years ago about to endure the supreme sacrifice. He grimaced but the closer she came the more convinced he became that, although she was being dramatic, there was also drama in certain irrevocable acts to which young maidens sometimes resort. With that thought in mind he backed into a dark corner and waited until she passed, then followed her at a discrete distance.

She went directly to her father's room and, after opening the top drawer to an old fashioned black walnut desk, took out an embossed leather case and opened it. Against the bronze plush lay two slim long-barreled dueling pistols. Not the puny kind generally used by so-called gentlemen who don't really wish to wound mortally, but deadly weapons of a hefty caliber. She found a cartridge, slipped it into the chamber and snapped the barrel back in place. It was then that Phil leaped from his hiding place and slapped the gun from her hand. Without word or preamble he sat in a chair, pulled her dress up above her buttocks and began to spank her with stinging, hard, full-armed sweeps that soon had her weeping and calling for him to stop in a loud voice.

"I should … injure you … in some mortal way … " He continued to spank until the room resounded with her cries.

He stopped and put her on her feet, her pose as she stood up making him bellow with laughter. One wrist covered her eyes and the other hand massaged her damaged behind; and the weeping continued.

"You stop laughing at me!" she screamed.

"Ah, we recover. Deldee, in all seriousness, it was a blow to discover that I was related to a fool. That I cannot abide and since I cannot change the relationship I took the only way open to rectify matters. Come now, change into something impractically seductive and we will catch the bus before it gets to Villa Enriquez."

"I won't," she sobbed. "I won't chase after him. If that's the way he is then that's the way he is and I won't … "

His hand smacked his leg with a sharp report, making her jump. "Come now, my little titmouse, and lets go run down your bull finch. An idea has been creeping in me for some time."

On the bus Don's spirits, already touching bottom, seemed determined to burrow beneath it like a mole.

He tried every sort of mental dodge known to man; he built castles, he stocked them with the most gorgeous women that mind could imagine; and every time Deldee would walk through the marble halls and leave the lot of them looking like hags. Finally, after three hours of furious effort, when capitulation was inevitable, he did the human thing and found an out.

It was now plain that Deldee was by all odds the most important thing in his life. To face the future without her was something he could not even imagine. When this thought was crystalized, weights tumbled from his back with such suddenness that he was moved to listen for the sound of an avalanche.

With a cry he leaped up in the aisle where he was promptly thrown into a fat woman and a huge basket of tortillas, enchiladas, and frijoles. Her screeches rent the air and the driver began to gesture with both hands and yell. Soon the whole bus was echoing to the lusty rendition of Spanish dudgeon and the welkin was ringing with a vengeance. Don managed to quiet the woman by forcing a hundred peso note on her but the driver was still unsatisfied and the others were still helping out.

"Stop!" yelled Don, brushing frijoles from his suit front with one hand and trying to drag his luggage with the other. "Stop! I want to get off."

"But Señor," screamed the driver, nearly letting the bus run over a cliff, "theese teeket she is for Villa Enriquez."

"I don't give a damn if it's for Acapulco. I'm getting off here and now. Stop the damn bus!"

The driver gave up with a shrug and stopped with such enthusiasm that Don tripped on his luggage and sprawled atop the fat woman, again reaping a barrage of infuriated Spanish which set the whole bus going afresh. He roduced another hundred peso note and her tirade turned instantly into a gold-toothed smile. The driver frowned and muttered something like, *"Gringo es loco en la cabeza."* Finally, after the accumulation of a great deal of dust, several lacerations and contusions, Don found himself on a lonely rocky road with a three thousand foot climb facing him.

He shouldered one bag and carried the other, remembering the times when he had carried two sea bags and an Ml rifle plus two hundred pounds of ammunition and a fifty-pound pack. The thought gave him scant comfort because the climb was tedious and before long, sweat had blinded him and his arms and legs were one continuous ache.

He saw the Sunbeam some distance up the grade as it whipped around a hairpin turn. But he chuckled dryly —he knew it for what it was. He had hoped for a car so intensely that he was seeing one in mirages, and as a mirage this one was a dilly because it even had sound effects.

Then before he had time to cogitate on the phenomenon the Sunbeam was upon him, had stopped and Deldee was running toward him sobbing his name. "Don... Don... You came back... you came back."

He dropped his bags and held her as though she were the last rock of firmament in a sea of destruction.

Phil smiled, lit a black cigarette and slumped in the seat for some time. Then he quirked an inquisitive eyebrow at them. "The average person would have to breathe once in a while, but when you're in love I suppose it's different."

They broke away and grinned at him; then, arm in arm, they came toward the car.

"Pardon me for putting in a word of crass materialism, but aren't your bags at all important?"

Don grinned sheepishly and went to fetch them.

They coasted down the long slope toward Telecos, the Sunbeam doing better with the bumps than had the bus. Phil was speaking. "So I was faced with a problem. Within the same month I had been dead wrong about two people. I had ascribed intelligence to them both that neither seemed to possess. That was a blow to my pride. I, the Great Soldarez, had been wrong. Imagine what a shock that was to my esthetic sensibilities. To one principal I was irrevocably related by blood. To the other I was no less strongly attached through a certain weakness I have for the lower orders. I—" He looked at them and saw that they were not in his world.

"I say—" Still no reaction from the huddle of humanity that was as close as was possible to get. "I say, you chaps—"

"Dammit," came the irritable reply. "Say it and be done with it."

Phil shrugged with Latin thoroughness and turned his attention to the road. "No appreciation," he said complainingly. "No appreciation for the finer aspects of the spoken word literately joined so as to make a sentence that swoops like a swallow, that glides like a kite—"

"And stinks like a buzzard," came the surprising reply.

Phil shrugged again. "No appreciation," he repeated. "However, there is a delightfully erected mouse I wot of who will listen with all evidence of rapt ... "

"Nuts," said a voice. "Circumstantial evidence."

Phil's face fell in lines of defeat and aimed the nose of the Sunbeam at the blocky bulk of his barracks. He ripped off three deadly bursts of imaginary machine gun fire, almost going in the ditch before he could release the trigger.

THE END

NOCHE DE AMOR

She walked out of the shadow toward him, her ripe hips undulating with such seductiveness that he felt as though he had touched a hot wire.

She stopped a few feet away and smiled slowly, her teeth white and clean in the dim light of the overhead bulb. She was a big girl and hefty in every department.

"Señor Don."

"That's me. But who are you?"

"I am Thereze."

Without intending to, he took a step backward. She seemed to blaze with a primordial hunger. It shone from the big dusky eyes, the satin smooth skin—from the whole attitude so unmistakable in intent that he felt a cool sweat break out on his brow. Her skirt was printed cotton, advertising the full contours.

"This is not an hour," he pointed out, "at which ladies visit gentlemen in their rooms."

She smiled wider, dimples pitting her cheeks. "I know that. I don't like a lot of women around when I visit."

www.ingramcontent.com/pod-product-compliance
Lightning Source LLC
Chambersburg PA
CBHW052007240626
47153CB00008B/2782